I0675334

# Switch

a novel

by Geoffrey Visgilio

2nd Edition

Copyright © 2017, 2019, Geoffrey Visgilio

This novel is entirely a work of fiction. The names, characters and incidents portrayed in it are the work of the author's fevered imagination. Any resemblance to actual persons, living or dead, events or localities is entirely coincidental.

ISBN-13: 978-1-7330709-1-1

This book is for me.

# Prologue

"SHE'S CHANGING," MILLER says. Pauses. "It's hard to explain."

Doctor Kendra leans forward in his chair, leathered brown hands directing Miller's gaze to the yin-yang medallion on the bookshelf.

"We get attached to someone with hopes they'll never change, but they always do, and so must we."

Miller is dismissive of Taoist fluffery.

"Look, it's not attachment or romantic delusions. That's not what I'm trying to say. It's…"

An encouraging nod from Doctor Kendra.

"…day-to-day stuff. Routine stuff. Does that make sense?"

The therapist considers him. A quick eye to the clock. Miller sees him. Doctor Kendra catches his eyes and smiles politely.

"You believe she's acting differently."

Miller nods.

"Give me an example."

Miller shakes his head, quickly, like shooing a fly away from his face and Doctor Kendra sees his patient has more than a few examples to choose from.

*Tell him about the bag.*

He feels goose bumps rise along his arms and knows Doctor Kendra will spot them immediately. He tucks his elbows into his crotch and leans forward on his forearms to cover.

*Tell him.*

His head shakes involuntarily again and he turns around for a quick peek at the clock. Three minutes left.

*Out with it.*

The impossible question: Can he trust Doctor Kendra? The physician watches him closely, seemingly sage behind dark eyes, but unknowable.

"The bathroom," he says, swallows. "That's the biggest one. It's hours in there. She never used to be like that. She'd take her time, sure. But this isn't getting-ready-to-go-somewhere time. She's camping out."

*That's not everything…*

"And…"

Doctor Kendra, expectant.

"Her speech is different." He changes course, he can't risk it yet; roundabout will still get you there. "She's been zoning out again. She-"

*She feels different. Tell him. Her skin feels different.*

"She feels-"

*Say it.*

"-distant."

*Pussy.*

Doctor Kendra surprises him.

"Do you believe that she may be ill?"

He had considered that, but in the end, his gut won out. Evelyn may be infected, but she wasn't sick.

"I don't think she's sick, I think she's *changing*."

Miller looks at the doctor, watching for signs of wariness behind his practiced gaze.

*Can I trust you, Kendra?*

He wrings his hands together.

*Here goes.*

"What does it take to get someone committed?"

An agonizing pause. Doctor Kendra, inscrutable, but Miller sees the wheels turning.

*Maintain eye contact. Breathe in through your nose.*

He can't stop wringing his hands.

"Miller."

Clinical, devoid of empathy. Miller's hands stop wringing.

*This was a mistake.*

"Do you believe she may be a danger to herself or others?"

*Tell him about the bag.*

Doctor Kendra's eyes dart to the clock.

*No time for more, herr doktor, this was a hit and run.*

The doctor smiles, drawing his lips down and out. But not up.

"You're tense," he says, rising and extending his hand. "You're jumping at shadows. Why don't you both come in next week and we'll talk about it. I'm afraid that's where we have to end things today."

Miller takes his hand. The handshake is genuine, but the doctor's eyes are shrewd, alert. Miller takes a deep breath in through his nose and exhales in a shudder.

"I know, it all sounds nuts."

*Smart.*

"You're right, I'm probably just jumping at shadows." Miller forces laughter and then just the right tone of schmaltz. "I just miss my wife."

Doctor Kendra pauses, disarmed. He smiles again and this time it catches, activating laugh lines, filling his eyes.

*Defused. Smart.*

"She misses *you*," he says. "We'll get there. All right?"

"All right, Doctor Kendra. Thank you."

There is an awkward turn-around, half-wave on the way out the door. But the doctor has already dismissed him, absorbed in his charts. Or pretending to be absorbed.

*Well, now you know for sure.*

He knew. Until he tested the waters, he could never really be sure in his stomach. But confirmation made his next moves easier. He could let go of hope. He couldn't trust Doctor Kendra, never again from this point forward. He was on his own. Perhaps that was for the best. Miller had finally made the decision to confront Evelyn before he came to therapy, he just wanted-

*I wanted you to go there with me, Kendra, God damn you. I wanted you to at least entertain the idea that it was possible. That she's gone. Kendra, you fuck.*

It didn't matter now. Too many things were in motion. Miller felt his nerves buzzing, cresting towards some unknowable crescendo. He was becoming sure of what had to come next. And Evelyn-

*It was Beasley in the bag.*

She was becoming something else entirely.

# Act I

"All the world is mad but me and thee.
And sometimes I wonder about thee…"

-Quaker saying

# 1

WHEN IT HAPPENED a second time, Evelyn was in the bathroom. The menstrual cramps had come on savagely and, despite a hearty handful of Motrin, she knew it was going to be a bad one. She'd left work early, beating Miller home by a couple of hours and promptly shut the curtains in the bedroom and collapsed onto the bed. She hoped Miller would be caught up in traffic, or would go and do a set at the club, and she could have peace for a while. She loved him, in her way, but he lurked when she wasn't feeling well and it made her crazy. His hovering attentiveness and his soft, reassuring voice jangled her nerves like a kid practicing the violin. Ugh, and that look, expectant, hopeful, like she was the sole source of his happiness.

Beasley, better trained than her husband, greeted her at the front door, butt wagging in spastic circles. But she passed the dog a sharp look and the wagging stopped. He whined softly and tucked his head down, retreating to another part of the house. She lay in bed, still in her work clothes, and tried to doze, but the cramps kept at her in rolling waves.

After about an hour, she felt the urge to urinate and worried for the third or fourth time that day whether she was getting a urinary tract infection. This game had been going on all afternoon – urgency, feelings of fullness in her bladder, pressure. But then, of course, she'd make it to the bathroom and nothing. She rolled onto her side, moaning and holding her belly, trying to will the sensation away. But trying to subdue it seemed only to embolden it. With great effort, she forced herself to get up.

The room spun and she lurched towards the bureau to steady herself. The image of her hand reaching out for the reassuring wood surface doubled and black spots bloomed at the sides of her vision. For a moment, she was sure she was going to pass out and split her head open on the corner of the dresser. *No more accidents for you, please.* Then her hand found the smooth surface and reality reasserted itself. She stood that way for a few minutes, breath ragged, coming out in harsh pants. She blinked the last of the vertigo out of her eyes.

"Am I getting sick?"

The sound of her voice made her jump. It was uneven and loud in the gathering dark of the bedroom. A shiver crept down the back of her neck and the skin at her palms began to sweat. Slowly, she removed her hands from the bureau and forced herself to walk unaided. The vertigo had passed, but that clammy feeling remained. One foot in front of the other, maneuvering like a sailor on land for the first time after a long stint at sea, she made her way to the bathroom.

She flicked on the light and went to the mirror, studying her face in the glass. Intensely blue eyes stared back at her, framed by a high forehead and cheekbones. She tried to smile, but it looked manic to her and she let her mouth relax. Her lips were thin and drawn seemingly forever downward. She had, what the girls at work called, a resting bitch face. She rarely smiled and when she laughed, it was a graceless thing, like the bray of a donkey, and she hated it. Miller used to make her laugh, used to thrive on it, and she indulged him despite her most strident efforts. But his toilet humor and his damnable puns and zingers had come to grate on her.

She frowned at the deepening crow's feet around her eyes and the lines around her mouth, once lightly etched and now carved, entrenched, into her face. She was pretty, she knew it, and despite these carvings as she leaned past thirty-two, she'd likely remain pretty all her life. She hated that too. Other women resented her and men became boldly lascivious around her. She hated the attention, unwanted, unjustified in her opinion. She hated people staring at her, drawn to a beauty she loathed like a deformity. She wished for anonymity, to pass unseen among people who would never know who she really was.

She shook dirty blonde hair out of her face, trying to banish the last of the unsteadiness from her head. She ran the tap and splashed cold water over her eyes and cheeks. She was debating drawing herself a hot bath when that sense of urgency caught hold again. She winced at herself in the mirror and cursed. Sighing, resigning herself to the demands of her biology, she slipped down her pants and panties and squatted over the toilet.

She looked down at her bare legs. The right one, puckered white with scar tissue over her knee and thigh, displayed ugly lines where she'd been cut apart by surgeons and reassembled with unforgiving metal pieces. The leg that still had numb spots and was terribly cold at night. The limp she would have the rest of her life. She touched her belly absently, feeling for a bulge that was no longer there. The accident, the injuries, she could somehow accept in her mind. Accidents happen. Wounds heal. But the absence? The inward curve of her belly? She didn't know if she'd ever get over that.

She closed her eyes and concentrated on relieving the pressure in her bladder. She imagined a swollen balloon filled with water slowly draining and collapsing in on itself. She was rewarded for her efforts by a trickle and then a stream of urine. It didn't burn, that was something. She leaned over on one thigh, craning her neck to look in the bowl. No blood, either, that was even better. Maybe it was just cramps and stress and it would all pass, like a fever dream seen to be ridiculous upon waking.

She was reaching for the roll of toilet paper when it started, a low hum. Waw-waw-waw-waw. At first she thought it was a headache, but the humming grew louder. It was distinctly coming from outside of herself. The overhead light flickered and dimmed, casting the bathroom into hectic shadows that frightened her. There was a sense of familiarity with this scene and a feeling of dread wrapped itself tightly around her guts.

"Oh no," she whispered.

Waw-waw-waw-waw. In time with her heartbeat, pounding at her temples. She tried to bring her breathing under control, but it was escaping her in sharp gasps. Panic was close.

"No," she whispered, more forcefully, spitting the words out. "Not again."

The bulb overhead flickered again and then beamed, the filament white hot, and she could smell the tangy stench of something burning. The light was bright enough to hurt her eyes. There was a loud popping sound as the bulb exploded and she instinctively brought her arms up around her head. The room was plunged into darkness.

Evelyn screamed.

\*\*\*

"Come on, Ev. Mom says you have to."

Evelyn eyed her older brother suspiciously. She hated the cellar, more than anywhere else, and Scott knew it well. Was this another in a long series of mean tricks he was pulling on her? A chance to send her down alone and lock the door behind her? She wouldn't put it past him, the rat. Just last week it had been the rubber snakes in her bed. How she had screamed. Scott, the rat, standing with his hands on his hips, delighted with his treachery. Her, fighting back tears of rage, hating him so much her hands shook.

"Aw Jesus, Ev," he had said. "Don't be such a baby."

She had to admit that Scott had taken a grudging interest in her lately and, despite his terrible ways of showing it, it felt better than being invisible. She was nine now and Scott had just turned twelve. For as long as she could remember, he had shunned her, mocked her, kicked her out of his room, ditched her every chance he got, and made her life a living hell if he was forced to babysit. It was only in the last year, since things had started growing visibly rocky in their parents' marriage, that he had come to tolerate her.

He never outright invited her to play with him or his friends, but he no longer chased her away when she followed him, and he'd toned down the ceaseless mockery when they were alone. She once overheard him talking to his friends from school about her. She'd followed him after the last bell to an old quarry the kids all played in. Tucked under some bushes, safely out of sight, she peered out at them, relishing the thrill of spying.

"She's okay," he had said. "Someone's gotta look after her."

Not a resounding endorsement, but she remembered how her heart filled and her cheeks burned red. She walked home, grinning ear-to-ear, and not even Scott's typical taunting later at dinner could dislodge that buoyant feeling. But this stank of a trick.

"I don't want to," she said.

Scott frowned down at her. He was always smiling, always laughing. A trickster. Her polar opposite. When he frowned he looked so adult, like their father – too serious. Any moment he'd start in with the baby insult. She hated *that*, more than anything else. She was closing in on double digits now and she'd stopped wetting the bed a long time ago – and God, if Scott ever found out about that, there'd be no end to it. She wanted his approval so badly, she ached for it. And babies got nothing from Scott but derision. Why did it have to be the cellar?

"I don't want to," she repeated. "It's scary."

The frown deepened. Their mother came into the kitchen with her pocketbook in hand. She looked hurried and annoyed, a look that had become a regular feature on her face as of late. They both knew better than to approach her for mediation, but Evelyn felt desperate.

"Mom," she said. "Tell Scott not to make me go into the cellar."

She scanned both of their faces, disinterested in the seeming peril that was growing in the kitchen. She sighed and looked down crossly at her daughter.

"I have to run to the food store," she said. "Your father is working late and I have to make dinner. Now Evvie, just go down and get the canned tomatoes."

"But *mom*." She was whining, she knew it, felt it in her voice, but was unable to stop. "Why can't Scott do it?"

Her mother was preoccupied, rooting around in her purse for the car keys.

"Scott has to finish his homework and I asked you to do it. Now please, Evvie, I don't have time for this."

Evelyn felt tears close and knew a scene would complicate matters. They were both staring at her now, her mother expectant, Scott sneering.

"Yeah *Evvie*," he mocked. "Don't be such a-"

She knew she'd go down to the cellar before the word was out and she balled up her fists and shouted at him.

"I'm not a baby!"

"Good," their mother said, voice clipped, already turning away from them. "Then it's settled. I should be back in an hour."

Scott grinned triumphantly at her and pointed to the cellar door. She heard the car start up and pull out of the garage and felt the last of her hopes go with it. Fists still balled at her sides, she headed for the door. She gripped the handle and twisted the knob, pulling with all her might. The door was slow to open and heavy on its hinges. A smell that made her think of open graves wafted up from the basement and she suppressed a shudder.

She flipped the lightswitch and a meager pool of light appeared at the bottom of the stairs. She looked over her shoulder at her brother.

"Just leave the door open, okay?"

He grinned again, nodding at her. It was a trick. She knew it for certain. She needed to be brave. Resigned to her fate, she trudged down the old stairs and into the maw of the cellar. The smell was worse down here, dank and musty, like a tomb. She knew there were bugs down here. She'd seen them, pale and squirming. The light cast most of the room into shadows. They were jagged shadows, warping the cranky boiler, the washer and dryer, and pieces of furniture covered in drop cloths into odd, unfamiliar shapes. A simple cluttered basement turned into a weird maze of potential monsters.

"Scott?" she called, but there was no answer from above.

She longed to stay in the pool of light from the lone bulb overhead, as weak as it was. But she knew the shelves with her mother's canning and preserves lined the far wall, deep in the shadows. She forced herself onward, moving past half-hidden lumps and strange bulk covered in cloth, seeming to reach out for her at lunatic angles. Three steps away from the back shelf, teasingly close to her objective, the light went out.

She wheeled around, terrified, and looked up the stairs at the welcoming light of the kitchen. She sprinted for it, barking her shin soundly on the corner of some hidden horror. She fell to her knees, gritting her teeth in pain as the window of light began to close. She forced herself up, breaking for the stairs, but the door swung shut with a resounding boom. She heard the deadbolt latch into place and Scott's tittering laughter from above. All around her was darkness.

Her shin throbbed and now there was a noise seeping out of the dark, a waw-waw-waw-waw sound like a nightmare's heartbeat. She told herself it was just the boiler, but it wasn't. This sound was different, alive somehow.

"Scott!" she screamed, climbing the stairs, feeling carefully for each step.

When she reached the top, she pounded on the door with all her strength.

"Scott! Let me out!"

She could feel him just on the other side of the door, could see his smug, self-satisfied grin in her mind's eye. The waw-waw-waw sound was getting louder and her tepid attempts to convince herself it was the boiler were unraveling. She pounded again, terror threatening to unhinge her. She tried the knob, and though it turned, she couldn't push past the deadbolt. She felt the darkness grow around her, seeming to move, now creeping up the first of the stairs to the kitchen.

It slipped up the steps, one by one, drawing closer, drawn by her frantic attempts at escape. Soon it would touch her. Something slick and impossibly old would reach around from behind and drag her down into the swallowing dark. And she would howl. She beat against the door, crying uncontrollably, tears running in hot rivers down her cheeks.

Her heart raced in her chest, in time with the humming that seemed to come from everywhere. She felt the first tendrils of horrible dark caress her shoulders and the last of her control broke apart.

"Scott!" she wailed. "*LET ME OUT!*"

There was a mighty crack, the sound of wood splitting. Then the deadbolt and the knob popped out and clattered to the tile on the kitchen floor. She pushed through the wreckage, face red, eyes burning, and emerged into the room. Scott was on the ground, propped up with his back against the fridge, staring up at her with wide eyes. The humming had stopped.

"The door…" was all he could say.

The floor was littered with the knob, the broken pieces of the deadbolt, and sharp splinters of wood. She turned back to face her brother and saw that he was visibly afraid. It was the first time she'd seen him like this in all their lives. She reached for him, protective, keenly aware, even at nine years old, that their roles had reversed. He scrabbled away from her, pointing at the deadbolt.

"You did that!" he blurted, awestruck.

She debated if she should simply agree with him and tell him if he ever made fun of her or called her a baby again, she could make his head explode. But she didn't have the stomach to be cruel to Scott, especially the way he was looking at her. He was afraid of her. All she wanted was to erase that awful look from his face. Besides-

"That's impossible," she said, matter-of-factly. "Don't be a doofus."

He shook his head, still incredulous.

"But what happened, Ev? What was that?"

16

She was honest.

"I don't know," she said. "But we better think what we're going to tell mom when she gets home."

That snapped him awake a little bit and he met her eyes. She reached for him again and this time he took her hand, letting her help him to his feet. They were on the same team. She never wanted to feel apart from him again. That look he gave her, like she was an outsider, a stranger, possibly dangerous, frightened her more than anything the darkness could conjure.

In the end, they decided to tell their parents that she chiseled the deadbolt out after the door had locked behind her by accident. The door, old wood swelled with the heat of the summer, had stuck fast and neither one of them could budge it. Scott, the hero of their concocted story, talked her through the whole thing, keeping her calm and steady while they busted her out of her subterranean prison. They had never shared a secret before, and despite the day's bizarre turn, that sharing was Evelyn's treasure.

Their father was proud of them, their mother muttered about old houses and safety. After some consideration and not a little fighting over costs, the old cellar door was replaced and all traces of the incident were cast off to the garbage heap.

*That's impossible*, she had said. But was it? Was it really? She wondered about that, a great deal more and for far longer than she'd ever admit. She and Scott never spoke of it again and despite his occasional pensive stares, he seemed content to let it drop.

Five years later, Scott was dead. Drowned in a lake. An accident. She'd been too small to save him. The funeral. The tears. The All-American tragedy. A boy cut down in his prime, months from a scholarship far away from their childhood home. Their parents' marriage fractured after that and she became invisible again behind their grief. With the only witness to that strange incident in the cellar gone, she let the loss chew away at her memories, like waves eroding the shore, until she all but convinced herself that it never happened in the first place.

Until the bathroom.

\*\*\*

She vaulted off the toilet, hiking up her pants, shaking glass out of her hair. The bulb had exploded with enough force, it shattered the outer housing of the light fixture. She tried the door, but it wouldn't budge. With increasing panic, she yanked as hard as she could, crunching glass under her feet, but the door was immovable. Defeated, shaken, she made her way to the corner of the bathroom. She cleared out glass underneath her and crouched down, nestling herself into the V of the walls.

*Waw-waw-waw-waw.*

She checked herself over for wounds, but found nothing sore or bleeding, though it was impossible to know for sure in the dark.

"Impossible," she said under her breath.

Her eyes adjusted to the dark and the familiar contours of the bathroom helped to dilute her fear. The thin sliver of light underneath the bathroom door promised her that the outside world was exactly where it was supposed to be. She traced the line of her scar through her pants and found resolve. No longer a frightened child locked in the cellar, now an adult in control, she worked to manage her breathing. After ten minutes, fiercely focused on the oasis of light under the door, her breath was even in her chest.

*Waw-waw-waw.*

She trained her focus on the handle of the door, projecting all of her concentration on the latch.

"Let me out," she said softly.

There was a grating noise and then a click. The door popped open and swayed outward, light stretching across the opening, glittering off the glass on the floor. She rose and brushed herself off, sighing with relief. She emerged from the bathroom, blinking in the hall light. The humming had stopped, so had her cramps, and her head felt light and clear. Her brother's voice echoed in her ears.

*You did that!*

She glanced at the bathroom door, into the darkness beyond, and felt something powerful stirring deep within her. She absently reached for her scar again.

"Don't be such a baby."

She grinned and headed for the pantry to find the broom and dustpan and some candles. She busied herself cleaning the bathroom, concocting a believable story for Miller when he got home. It wasn't the first lie she'd told in the five years they'd been married, but she sensed intuitively that it was important she stand by it.

She had a secret to protect.

# 2

MILLER WAS SWEATING a little onstage, but he was killing it.

"Do you guys have that one friend on Facebook who likes *everything* you post? No matter what it is?"

The crowd was rumbling. There was a sway to them, their laughter was freer and louder and everyone was three or four beers deep. They were riding his wave. This was Miller's favorite part.

"No matter what you post?"

The laughs were good ones.

"Pot roast for dinner."

A guy in the front row grinned.

"Go you!" he shouted in his best Valley Girl voice.

They chuckled.

"Man, I hate dentists."

"Dentists are such meanies! Feel better hun. LOL."

He tittered in a high falsetto.

"Like no matter what you put up there, this person is your Japanese schoolgirl, notebook clasped to her chest, *superfan*. It's UNREAL."

He shook his head and grinned at the floor. He looked back up at them and saluted.

"I've joined the Nazi party."

He put his thumbs up and beamed.

"You crazy man!"

He shook his head again.

"I enjoy frequenting prostitutes."

Thumbs up again.

"You scamp!"

They were ready for the closer, so he grabbed the microphone and brought it close to his lips for the muffled sound.

"I ATE A BABY."

"Yay! No child support!"

He started to laugh at himself at that last one and they caught his wave and it rolled, like summer whitecaps. He grabbed the mike with both hands and belted the rest out.

"It's always so cute, you know? Like they're unstoppable, you know? Like even if you called them out on it and said: YOU! You're the one, you're *relentless*. They'd totally fucking agree with you!"

He rolled his eyes.

"Oh my God, I totes do that! LMFAO."

The girl voice killed every time; he took generous liberties with it.

"Like you could fucking shake them, right?"

He made a constipated face and shook the microphone stand like he was trying to throttle it.

22

"And scream, and say: every post! I can't keep up! You're *literally* killing me. I can't take it. WHAT DO YOU WANT FROM ME?"

They were full with it now and he was laughing and they were laughing and it was open. The channel between them was clear and everyone in the room was vibrating just on the lip of an unfathomable apex. He twisted his index finger into his cheek, opened his eyes wide, and grinned at them.

"I just want you to LOVE ME, POOKIE BEAR!"

He shook his neck and gave them the crazy eyes.

"FOREVER!"

The light blinked twice in the back. Nailed it. Timing like a Swiss watch.

"That's all the time I have, folks, thanks very much!"

He bowed, letting his knuckles fall to the hardwood. The thump. A new ritual. How he knew it was over. He rose to wolf whistles and loud clapping. He put a hand over his heart and bowed his head. The thunder of them was like a blanket, soft and good to snuggle under. He waved, their applause carried him off.

She watched him go. It was the second night she'd come to see him. She liked his voice, his energy. He was having fun with it, it wasn't a routine. It played like it was unrehearsed. He was natural. He knew what made people tick. And he was clever. That thing he said, that first night, about fool's destiny, it stayed with her. He was serious then, for just a moment. She didn't plan on coming to see him again. She didn't plan on marrying him.

And she certainly didn't plan on the chair.

\*\*\*

She stirs, coming more awake by degrees. The kitchen has been cleaned out. The table broken down and stuffed into the back walkway. The extra chairs piled in another room. Centerpiece, tablecloth, appliances on the counter, jars, knives: everything is gone. She has no idea where. In their place, a roll of duct tape, some tools, a handgun, and a pack of cigarettes in a glass ashtray on top of the stove.

No alcohol in sight, that was in her favor. All that remained was her damnable chair and an empty one, face-to-face, open space between them. The light cover has been removed from the overhead. A bare bulb glares from a socket in the ceiling. An interrogation? A quick glance to the counter. Or worse? For the first time since she awoke, she struggles in the chair, but she is taped fast at her wrists and ankles. She hears footsteps come down the hall. Miller enters the kitchen and squats down in front of her. He looks up at her, like stone, ready for the work ahead.

The bald gravity of the situation collapses upon her.

"Gotcha," he says.

\*\*\*

"You don't seem like you laugh very often," he said.

He caught her, exposed her. She looked down sharply and then away. But she was quick on the return and gave him a smile that turned Miller's insides into liquid.

"Not everyone can be a funnyman like you."

He tapped his chin, felt a fidget coming on, and reached for a sip of his drink. The bar was watching, subtly, quietly, but they were watching just the same.

"So you're saying we all have roles to play?"

She sat back, smoothing her jacket and skirt as if to agree with him.

"Duties," she paused. "Responsibilities."

"So you're saying I'm irresponsible?"

"No," she leveled her eyes at him. "I'm saying our priorities are different."

He squinted at her, studying her. It was a long stare, she was beginning to feel uncomfortable and then, very softly.

"Who hurt you?"

She recoiled, narrowed her eyes, and glared at him. Here it comes. But then the corner of his mouth twitched and there was a twinkle at his eyes and then she was laughing before she could stop herself. It was a good one too, from her belly, ungracious and genuine. It was a different laugh, separated from the others. For him alone. He spread his hands out.

"There you go," he said. "Let it out."

She smiled at him.

"So you're a therapist now?"

He shook his head.

"I just know when people are taking themselves too seriously."

She laughed again, an audience of one, and deflated, leaning into the bar, relaxing into herself as best she could. She turned on him.

"I need to chill, huh?"

He put his hand up to the bartender.

"This will help," he said. "But since you're the responsible one here, lady, you get this round."

He gestured to the seat beside him and turned to order them drinks. She climbed onto the stool and looked at him.

"Lady?"

He shrugged.

"It's not lady," she said and extended her hand. "It's Evelyn."

"Jesus," he said and took her hand. "No wonder you're so fucking tense."

She retracted her hand and slapped him on the shoulder. He used his finger to push his nose up and did his best Jeeves for her.

"Now presenting, the Lady Evelyn. Presumably, her farts do not smell."

She ignored him.

"Do they make a sound?"

She covered her mouth with her hand.

"Or are they just a little puff, like a dog fart?"

Another hit on the shoulder. He leaned into her.

"Do you just lean to the side and it's a little, tiny squeak…."

She nudged him away. He fought to stay. She let him. This is how it all got rolling.

***

How had he gotten the jump on her? She remembers sitting at dinner with him in the kitchen. He'd been pensive, more so than usual, watching her carefully. It's a look she'd grown accustomed to lately, but there had been more. He had been uncomfortable, speaking hurriedly, rushed in his movements. The drink. It must have been the champagne.

*Down the hatch!* He had drugged her. Where had he gotten drugs like that? More to the point, how long had he been planning this? How long had her husband been keeping his own secret from *her*?

She remembers sounds in the darkness, shuffling and scraping she now understands was furniture getting cleared out. And there had been a ripping sound, which she now knows was duct tape, fixing her solidly to the chair. The damned chairs. Miller's mother's. Hardwood relics from the fifties, they were scuffed and battered, but terrifically sturdy. She hated them, ugly artifacts of a bygone era, but anything to do with Miller's mother was a touchy subject on the best of days, so she'd grudgingly accepted them among their collected things. Now this.

She passes a quick look to the gun on the stovetop and back to Miller. He is pacing, left to right, in front of her, watching her. His look is steady, curious, detached, like he's observing some deadly animal behind the thick glass of a zoo enclosure. The pacing means he is not in control however, that he hasn't fully summoned the nerve yet for what she suspects is a dirty job ahead. She recognizes opportunity in his instability, though she doesn't know if she can reason with him like this. He is so grim, hard, and underneath, the sting of betrayal pulses through him like a fever. For now, she decides, silence is the most sensible option.

She looks to the gun again. She can't help it. *Her* gun – there's the rub. She'd seen Miller violent, erratic, drunk and raving, but was he capable of murder? Of murdering *her*? There was a finality to the gun – *her gun* – that raised the stakes to a whole new level. It wasn't that Miller had a

27

secret, it was that he'd made a decision. Somewhere deep inside himself, he'd crossed a line. Or was ready to cross it. Maybe there was still time. Maybe-

"Look at me," he commands, voice empty of all compassion.

He doesn't speak her name. There is no invitation, no commonality, just the order. She obeys him.

"If you try and scream for help," he points to the roll of duct tape on the stove. "I'll gag you. If you try and struggle, I'll hurt you. Do you understand?"

There was contempt, rumbling deeply through his voice. And was there fear?

"Miller," she attempts. "Why are you doing this?"

He holds up a hand to her, it is shaking slightly.

"Do you understand?"

She nods.

"Good," he says and settles into the chair across from her. "Now I need answers from you. And you're going to give them to me. You should know I'm prepared to do what it takes to get the truth."

He stares at her, pitiless.

"You don't have to do this," she repeats. "Miller. *Please.* It's me. It's your wife. I'm Evelyn."

He sneers at her, teeth bared, and she is finally afraid.

"You're not Evelyn."

She feels something deep in her belly drop like a stone.

***

"So, is this…" she paused. "What you do?"

He laughed at her, expansive and welcoming, and she envied that. Instantly and painfully, she envied his openness and the ease of his humor. She had been constrained for as long as she could remember. She suddenly felt like he was so far out of her league, they may as well be on different continents. She balked at this idea. Surely she wasn't attracted to this ridiculous man, with his shaggy hair and unkempt appearance? But that laugh? It was welcoming, alive, and his eyes were warm and kind.

"Not a respectable job, being an amateur comedian? Eh?"

She fingered her glass, unsure of what to say, regretting she'd asked him the question. The silence drew out and she feared she offended him. Stupid, she was stupid.

"Actually, I'm a counselor," he said. "For abused and abandoned kids."

She turned to face him.

"Not what you expected, right?"

She nodded, trying to picture him behind a desk, attempting to put broken children back together again.

"So this is how you blow off steam?" she asked.

He grinned at her.

"Yeah, something like that."

He looked out across the bar and she sensed she was treading into overly personal territory, but she couldn't retreat.

"How did you get into a line of work like that?" she asked.

He laughed again, but there was a bitterness to it that she didn't like.

"My mother's crazy," he said.

He was smiling at her, but she could see pain and hurt behind his eyes. Before she knew what she was doing, she reached her hand across the bar, grasped his, and squeezed. He looked down at her hand, surprised, and she wondered if he might pull free and make some excuse to get away from her. But he squeezed back and they sat in comfortable silence for a few moments.

"And you, Lady Evelyn? Do the fartless work or just lounge around all day?"

"I work, thank you very much," she said primly, producing a business card from her jacket and passing it across to him.

He tapped the card and looked her up and down.

"What?" she asked.

"No surprises here," he said.

She pulled her hand away from his and took a slug from her drink.

"And what's that supposed to mean, funnyman?"

"Event coordinator?" he asked. "Someone likes to control the action, methinks."

She frowned at him.

"Are you analyzing me again, Doctor?"

He shook his head.

"No way," he said. "I just call 'em like I see 'em."

The bartender made his way over to them. Evelyn paused for a moment, hesitant, and then nodded for another round.

"So how does a sharply dressed event coordinator find her way into a shitty comedy club like this one then?" he asked.

"Conference," she said. "The guy at my hotel said you were all pretty funny down here."

"And the rest of your conference folks?"

She shrugged.

"Out at the bars, or some bimbo nightclub probably."

He nodded.

"Not your scene?" he asked.

She shook her head.

"Not my people."

He looked at her for a long while. She brushed hair away from her cheek, embarrassed.

"What?"

"I think there's a lot more to you, Lady Evelyn, than you let on."

"Think so, do you?"

They held eyes, longer than she knew they should, and she felt a flutter in the pit of her stomach.

"Your hotel," he said. "Does it have a nice quiet bar in the lobby?"

A blush rose in her cheeks. This was the part where she paid for the drinks, made some fumbling apology about having to show up at the conference early, and took her exit. But something in him, beyond his boldness and the cavalier way he carried himself, made her want to stay in his space as long as she could. What was it he said last night?

*A fool's destiny is to always be surprised.*

"Maybe," she said.

But the answer was yes. She knew it was yes from the moment she sat down.

\*\*\*

He rises from his chair, like he can't stand to look at her face any longer, and resumes pacing. She chances a glance behind her as he gets up – the shades in the kitchen are all drawn down. No hope of rescue from the outside then.

"I want to know what you did to Beasley."

"I didn't do anything."

"You're lying!" he thunders.

"Miller, I don't know what you're talking about. You need to listen to me now, okay? This has gone too far. You need to let me go."

"*What did you do to the fucking dog?*" he screams.

His voice is deafening in the empty room. She recoils. His fury is terrifying.

"Honey, *please*. Stop this."

He turns mid-stride, like a soldier on a parade ground, and stalks to the stove. She struggles against her bindings now, anticipating pain. He looks over the things scattered there and finally pulls the pack of cigarettes out of the glass ashtray. With a deep, tortured sigh, he plucks one free from the pack. He produces a lighter from his pocket, holds it under the cigarette, and then lights it. He sucks the smoke in deep, closing his eyes. He turns to her.

"Did you kill Beasley?" he asks, voice even.

She is incredulous.

"What? No! What's wrong with you?"

He sighs again, returning his gaze to the stovetop. He runs his free hand over the collection of tools, finally settling over a hammer. He picks it up, examines it, and returns to sit back down in the chair across from her, holding it out to her like an accusing finger.

"I'm going to ask you again. Did you kill Beasley?"

Could she explain it to him? Could she even try? She had loved that dog, loved him more intensely than her own husband at times. He was the closest thing she'd ever get to another child and she would have done anything for him. How could he ever comprehend that? The sheer depth? The almost madness of her love? And here it was, no longer in the shadows, but right out in front of her face. All the while she'd been…what? *Changing*. All the while he'd been plotting against her, steeling himself for torture and murder.

Suddenly she is angry, furious. All of her fears are eclipsed by white-hot rage. This is how it has always been, since the dawn of time. Men. With pitchforks and torches and self-righteous brutality, eager to dominate and destroy, to pillage and rape and burn to the ground all they cannot understand. How much mystery has fallen under their boot heels? How much wonder has been crushed underfoot by the march of progress? She strains against her bonds again, driven by hatred, for his gender, for its clumsy caveman stupidity, and for her own subjugation.

"Yes!" she shouts. "I killed him! And if you so much as touch me with that thing, I swear to God I'll kill you too."

She expects something from him – rage, fear, some level of apprehension. But the icy look he gives her is far worse. She feels her anger slapped away from her in an instant.

"You're going to kill me?" he asks, hefting the hammer. "We'll see about that."

# 3

MILLER HATED BEASLEY from the moment he saw him, shaking his self-important ass in the kitchen. That stupid curly-cue tail. A wiggly turd with a face thunked flat by the Good Lord's shovel. A pug! Of all the dogs.

*Four hundred fucking breeds of dog in the world, Evelyn, and this is what you pick…*

It turned on him in its weird half-wiggle, half-hop, and stared up at him with bugged-out black eyeballs. The dog never stopped moving, like a deranged wind-up toy. He grinned, slobbered, and barked. Miller looked up.

"No."

But she'd already gone coo-coo, he could see it.

"He wants you to pet him, Miller."

The dog pivoted, trying to love them both at the same time, and Miller couldn't shake the image of some kind of windup bouncy infant toy that just kept going. There was an on-off switch somewhere, hidden from a child's prying fingers, and maybe if the damned thing would stop moving for a second, you could find it. It was mesmerizing.

"No," he repeated.

She ignored him.

"Come on," she goaded. "Beasley wants you to say hi."

The dog pawed at his ankles, whining softly.

"Don'cha, Beasley?"

Beasley flipped out, digging into Miller's shins with his front legs like a steam shovel. If he stood there much longer he was going to be an asshole to both Evelyn and this dog. The fingers in his right hand twitched involuntarily and he knew she'd won. He felt his knees bend and the dog was upon him. He had a vision flash across his mind: standing hip-deep in snow with this wiggling turd passing more of itself out into the world in negative temperatures, while the orange sliver of an icy dawn split the sky. He pointed a finger up at Evelyn.

"This is not my dog," he warned. "This is your dog."

She smiled.

"Beasley is *our* dog."

Beasley, who didn't seem to care either way, snuffed at them. It was all over.

***

"Honey, he's making the face, better get him out."

Three weeks since Evelyn brought the dog home and their little rental house in the suburbs looked like a warzone. Dog toys were strewn about, seemingly sentient and mischievous, rolling underfoot to trip them up after dark. Newspaper covered the floor to the front entrance, the back porch, and the side door to the garage to catch mishaps. A crate had been purchased to train Beasley, but that had lasted all of two nights before his incessant whining made Evelyn cave.

"He has to learn, Lyn," he had said.

But the dog was already in bed with her and they were both looking at him with earnest, pleading eyes. Miller tried a dogbed, but with the permission given once, Beasley now understood the bed was part of his domain. He trotted happily in dizzy circles, first one way, then another, digging into the comforter until he'd made a suitable spot at the foot of their bed. Contented, he collapsed down and proceeded to lick himself in loud snuffles.

Puppyproofing the house proved a slipshod affair, the two of them continually adapting as Beasley destroyed something new. First came a nasty lemon-smelling spray for the sockets and wires after Miller caught him chewing through the cord to the electric blanket in their bedroom. Then came flip hooks for the closets after he made short work of a pair of Evelyn's favorite Michael Kors pumps. Heavy knickknacks were removed from high shelves as Beasley's bouts of 3a.m. mania found him banging off bookcases and cabinets like a pinball.

Things had finally settled out after the first few weeks, but potty training was still proving to be touch and go. They tried to put Beasley on a schedule, taking him out twice a day and crating him while they were at work, but the dog's bladder and bowels defied regiment. After a series of accidents and an assortment of cleaners – *this hippie crap doesn't work, Lyn, where's the bleach?* – they had come to recognize a mix of consideration and slack-jawed puzzlement that would cross Beasley's face before he piddled or shat. What followed was a comedic mad dash to hustle the dog out the door before the inevitable.

"Miller, hurry!"

He grabbed the dog under one arm like a football and bolted for the front door. She sprinted past them and opened it, waving them through like a traffic cop. He crossed the threshold and practically tossed Beasley onto the front lawn, already checking his shirt and his pants for the telltale signs that they hadn't been fast enough. When he turned back, the dog was bee-lining it for the nearest tree in his dizzying half-wiggle, half-hop. One little back leg went up and the dog voided his bladder, seemingly unfazed by all the drama. Evelyn came up behind Miller with the leash in her hands and handed it to him.

"Score one for the good guys," she said and kissed him on the cheek.

Beasley was kicking dirt and grass over his leavings with his hind legs, barking at them with delight. This was the new normal.

\*\*\*

"Miller!" she screamed. "Come quick."

He blinked, still half-in and half-out of a dream. He grumbled, rolling over to see what all the fuss was about, but Evelyn's side of the bed was empty. She screamed again, more urgently, and that brought him fully awake. He'd heard his wife scream maybe a handful of times in their time together and this wasn't anger or surprise – she was afraid. He sprang out of bed, fumbling for his glasses on the nightstand. He tripped over a squeaky toy on the way out of the bedroom and cursed loudly.

He rushed down the stairs to the source of the screaming and found Evelyn standing over Beasley in the living room, both hands pressed over her mouth. She was trembling.

"Lyn, babe, it's the middle of the-"

She pointed. The dog was on his side, breathing in labored grunts. There was shit everywhere and a mix of drool and blood collected in a pool under Beasley's head. He looked up at them, whining, seemingly in terrible pain. The smell hit Miller and he choked down a gag. The diarrhea was foul, and there was a perfume of sickness to it that they'd never experienced before.

"What happened?" he asked her.

She said nothing, only stood motionless, staring down at the dog with wide, horrified eyes.

"Lyn," he said and came over to her. "What happened?"

Still frozen, she worked her mouth, but nothing came out.

"Babe," he said and shook her by the shoulders.

Her eyes cleared and she blinked at him.

"What happened?" he repeated.

"I…" she stammered. "I don't know."

He stared at her, then down at Beasley, and knew whatever happened next, it was all on him. He snapped into action.

"I'm going to call the vet hospital and let them know we're coming. His papers are upstairs in the filing cabinet where we keep the taxes. There's car blankets in the garage, above the paint stuff. Can you grab those and lay them out on the backseat?"

She nodded, but she wasn't listening.

"Evelyn!" he shouted.

But now the tears were coming and her trembling had turned into the shakes. He moved, leaving her standing over the dog. He raced into the garage, flipping on the lightswitch, and scanned the shelves. He grabbed a tarp and some heavy blankets and made a makeshift bed for Beasley in the back of their SUV. He took another blanket and brought it back into the living room and threw it over the corner of the couch. He ran upstairs, flipping on lights as he went, rummaging through their important papers until he found Beasley's vet info. He made a quick stop to their bedroom to grab his phone and called the hospital.

Back in the living room, he pushed past Evelyn and grabbed the blanket. He leaned over Beasley.

"Okay, buddy, just hang on, I'm gonna wrap you up."

He reached under the dog and lifted him as gently as he could, ignoring the smell, the feverish heat, and the terrible panting. Beasley whined, but didn't fight back, and Miller settled him into the blanket, wrapping him up as gently as he could. He rose, bundle in both arms, and looked at Evelyn. She looked lost.

"Hey," he directed. "Grab those papers and we'll take him."

She shook her head slowly, still in a daze.

"Someone has to stay to clean this up," she said, voice barely above a whisper.

He looked down at the mess on the rug, then leaned in so he could look her directly in the eyes.

"Lyn, listen to me. Beasley needs you. And I can't do this alone."

She glanced down at the panting bundle in his arms and her eyes filled with fresh tears.

"Lyn," he insisted. "Please."

He nodded over to the papers and she finally got moving. He carried Beasley out to the garage and settled him into the backseat. He started the truck and honked twice. Evelyn got in, clutching the folder of papers and a stuffed alligator tightly to her chest. She held it up to him.

"I thought..." she said. "I thought he might want his little friend..."

The rest was lost in sobs. Miller leaned over her and buckled her in, pulling the SUV out of the driveway and speeding down the road to the vet hospital. He put the pedal to the floor, gunning through stop signs and red lights, repeating the same phrase, like an urgent mantra.

*It's going to be okay. It's going to be okay. It's going to be okay.*

\*\*\*

Even at three in the morning, the animal hospital was a rush of activity. The nervous barks of dogs and the angry yowls of cats rose into a cacophony of fear and suffering. Under the harsh lights, everyone had the same drawn and listless faces, drained of color, with heavy bags under their eyes, the faces of expectant people waiting for news. There was a wild smell to the place, like a barn, punctuated by the harsh tang of antiseptic.

Beasley had been rushed into the back by the attendant and Miller filled out paperwork while Evelyn paced in nervous circles around the counter. They reviewed Beasley's vaccinations while one of the vet techs solemnly explained that Beasley's symptoms were in line with those of parvo or distemper. All they could do was wait until the vet could see them, which given the bustle of the place, might take a while. Miller led Evelyn to a pair of uncomfortable plastic chairs away from the other pet owners and sat quietly with her while they waited.

Over two hours had passed and Evelyn rested her head onto Miller's shoulder. The crying had stopped, but she was sullen and heavy with grief. Miller had tried to flip through some magazines, but the pictures of grinning puppies and playful cats only made things worse. He gave up after a while and stared at the door to the back rooms, willing the vet to come and bring them some good news.

"He's going to die," she breathed into his shoulder.

"What?"

"Beasley," she said. "He's going to die."

He turned and brought her into his arms so he could hold her.

"Don't talk like that."

"He is," she persisted.

He put his hands around her face and turned her up to look at him. Her eyes were glassy and the skin around them was puffy from crying. The frownlines around her mouth had deepened and her nostrils were wet with mucous. She looked worn out, but that could be remedied with some hot food and a good night's sleep. It was the hollow certainty behind her eyes that Miller was worried about.

"Why would you say that?"

"Because everything I love dies."

Miller knew better than to say anything else. Things had been hard for them, too hard he believed for most couples to bear. Her affair (*It was just a fling, Miller. Jesus!* Like that made it any better.) had assaulted him. It weakened his confidence, eroded his faith in enduring love. And a tumble down a flight of stairs had all but extinguished the last of Evelyn's joy. The recovery had been harrowing, aging them both, hardening them both. And the shock of losing their child. Of losing…

Even now, after therapy and meds and the slow, arduous process of learning to love each other again, he still couldn't mention the name.

He couldn't stand it. This was too much. Beasley was healing them, wasn't he? In silly and ardent measure, he had brought the sun back streaming into a dusty, unused room. Damned if he was going to surrender into defeat now.

"Listen to me, Lyn," he said. "That little shitloaf has grown on me and I'm not going to give up on him now. And neither are you. You get me?"

She nodded and tried to smile.

"He's going to be eating more of your shoes and every power cord we have in no time. Okay?"

She nodded again, the smile sitting easier on her face.

"I swear to God, you brought home a fucking beaver and not a dog."

She laughed. It was a choky thing, more a spasm than a laugh, but it sounded like music to Miller's ears. He tucked his bottom lip under his front teeth and made a beaver face at her, chomping at her nose. She swatted him away and some of the life returned to her eyes.

"Mr. Coretti?"

The attendant had come out; she was holding the door to the back exam rooms open.

"You can come back now."

Evelyn gripped his arm tightly.

"Come on. We gotta go."

He rose. She resisted him at first, holding fast to his arm. But he brought her to her feet and took her hand in his. Together, they walked through the doors to the exam room.

\*\*\*

Beasley lay on a blanket on the metal examination table. He wiggled and tried to get up when he saw them come in, but he was too weak. Part of his front paw had been shaved down and a small IV was pumping a clear liquid into his system. They surrounded him and he licked their hands weakly. The veterinarian was a small, severe-looking woman in her mid-forties, with piercing eyes and kinky, curly hair tamed by a ponytail.

"Well," she said. "I've got good news. We ran some tests and it's not parvo. Or distemper. And there's nothing in his test results to suggest he ingested anything poisonous."

She patted Beasley's head affectionately.

"It looks like he just caught a nasty virus. Pretty common between boosters, actually. Scary, but he's going to be okay."

Miller let out the breath he'd been holding in a rush and scratched behind Beasley's ear.

"Thank Christ," he said.

Evelyn pointed to the IV, still not convinced.

"Fluids," the vet said. "He's pretty dehydrated. Diarrhea will do that. We're giving him anti-virals by injection right now. You're going to have to follow up with pills for a week or so when you take him home."

"When will that be?" Evelyn asked.

"I want to keep him overnight, but you should be able to pick him up tomorrow. Okay?"

Evelyn looked to Miller. He nodded and put his hand out. The doctor took it and he shook her hand.

"Thank you, Doctor."

The vet turned to Evelyn, hand extended, but she rushed forward, hugging her tightly, knocking her back a few steps. After an awkward moment, she embraced Evelyn and patted her on the back.

*Score one for the good guys.*

\*\*\*

Three weeks after that night, Beasley was back to his old self. Miller had breezed through his casework one Friday and left the office early. He let him out of his crate and they'd taken a stroll to the dog park. After some meet-and-greet and a copious amount of butt sniffing, Beasley was treated to a bone from the butcher shop and Miller drove them back home. There, he let Beasley run amok while he retreated to his study so he could work on a new bit for his act.

He was half-listening to the Red Sox game on the radio when the dog padded in and dropped his favorite stuffed alligator at his feet – the universal sign for, *play with me.*

"Oh man, dog," Miller said. "You just can't get enough today, huh?"

Beasley whined up at him and pushed the gator closer to Miller's feet with his snout. He seemed to understand that it was Miller who had taken charge the night he was sick and had become extremely affectionate towards him. He would dutifully carry his leash to Miller when it was time to go out and usually wound up in his lap at night when they would watch television. Evelyn feigned insult at this, but she was also grateful that he had been so strong that night. Despite Miller's best protests, Beasley was steadily becoming *his* dog, whether he liked it or not.

He reached down for the alligator. Beasley pounced on it, clamping its head in his little jaws and snarled. Miller grabbed the tail and shook. The dog held on, wiggling with delight, and dug his feet into the carpet, trying to pull away. They wrestled like this, Miller eventually crouching down on all fours, chin on the carpet, eye-to-eye with his opponent. He finally snatched the toy away and held it just out of reach from Beasley's frantic jaws.

"Sit," he said.

The dog looked at him, drooling out of the side of his mouth, and barked.

"Sit."

Beasley eyed the toy, then Miller, and parked his rump on the carpet.

"Good boy!"

He barked again. Miller rose and held the gator up over Beasley's nose. He spun it in circles around his face. Beasley nipped at it, barking. Miller held it higher and Beasley got up on his hind legs to chase after it. He shook it in an arc and the dog spun on his hind legs, trying to follow the toy. Miller laughed.

"Thatta' boy. Dance like no one's watching!"

He wound up and pitched the gator across the room. Beasley tore after it. Miller looked up at his desk, giving in to the fact that he would get no more work done today. The dog returned and Miller sprawled out on his back, arms at his sides. Beasley jumped onto his chest, dropped the drool-covered alligator on him, and lolled his tongue at him.

"No!" Miller said, but the tongue was at his face in no time flat.

He threw the alligator again, but Beasley would not be swayed and gobbled at his face with delight. He put his hands up, fighting the onslaught, and finally pushed the dog off him, rolling up onto his side. Evelyn stood in the doorway, watching them. He wiped his face and rose to meet her.

"Hey," he said. "I didn't know you were home."

"I caught you," she said, teasing.

He shook his head.

"I was…we were just fucking around."

She looked down at Beasley, who barked up at her in welcome.

"You were playing with him."

"I was not."

"You *love* him."

"I do not."

She stepped in to close the distance between them and kissed him deeply.

"Wow," he said when she finally pulled away. "What was that for?"

"For being you," she said, working on the drawstring of his sweatpants.

They hadn't been intimate in a long time. There had been a couple of close calls, most that had ended in either her tears or his anger, but this felt natural and sweetly overdue, like finding someone he thought he'd lost a long time ago.

"Hi," she said, grasping at the base of him.

"Hi," he breathed, finding the nape of her neck.

She squeezed and his breath quickened.

"I've missed you," he said.

"Show me."

There was a flurry of clothing, urgency, sighs and pleasure. Beasley, seemingly embarrassed, escaped the room, leaving the lovers to their embrace.

# 4

THE ASH ON Miller's cigarette is growing long. She nods over to it, trying to distract him from the hammer in his lap. He follows her gaze, blinks as if he's forgotten all about it, and rises from the chair, leaving the hammer on the seat. He cups his free hand under the ash, mindful of making a mess, and walks over to the ashtray. This stirs something in Evelyn, his seeming fuss over making a mess, still surprisingly courteous of his wife's tidy kitchen. Blood spatter is okay, but ashes are a big no-no. At any other time, it would be funny, but Evelyn doesn't feel much like laughing.

"When did you start smoking again?" she asks.

He takes a drag, looks down at the butt for a long moment, then stabs it out in the ashtray.

"Few weeks ago," he says. "Give or take."

"Why now?"

He throws his arms up into the air and glares at her.

"Kind of an intense situation here, Lyn."

He is using her name again, that's a good sign. Maybe she can salvage something out of this situation if she is careful.

"You were doing so good."

He laughs and stares at her, eyes wide.

"Like it matters now!" he shouts. "Look around you! You think we're going back to happily ever after once this is over? You think Doctor Kendra can mediate this?"

"Miller," she says calmly. "You can stop this. You don't have to-"

"No!" he snaps, slamming his hand down on the counter. "There's no going back now."

She wants to see where he is, how far he is willing to go, but now she is afraid to know.

"What are you talking about?"

He gives her an empty look, resigned, like the very last of the man she used to know has been poured out.

"I'm going to find out what I need to know from you. And then…"

He stares at the gun, speaking as if she is no longer in the room. It is then she knows there is no salvage possible, not now, not ever. Even before he finishes, she understands what comes next is irrevocable.

"Then I'm going to kill us both."

\*\*\*

She woke in the morning, after their first night in the club, uncertain for a moment where she was. She rolled and found Miller, still asleep, snoring softly, peaceful in the light of the dawn. She expected the pangs of regret, the slutty feeling of doing something impulsive and out of character, but there was instead a giddy thrill that made her toes tingle and her cheeks warm. She wanted to reach out and touch him, to brush that sloppy mop out of his face so she could look at him, but she was afraid if she did, the illusion would shatter and she would find herself in a strange hotel bed alone.

He stirred and she felt the secret moment collapsing. She was suddenly embarrassed for him to see her exposed, naked, with no makeup, no cloud of alcohol to soften their edges. Her first impulse was to run to the bathroom and lock the door, but he was blinking and then-

"Well hello there," he said, voice still thick with sleep.

She scrutinized his face, looking for rejection or dismissal or some form of sober regret for taking her to bed. But he only grinned at her, a sloppy half-grin that was easy on his face and reminded her of a young Harrison Ford.

"Hello, funnyman."

He reached out to stroke her cheek and she forced herself to not flinch.

"What is it?" he asked.

His hand was hot and strong and that giddy feeling was warring with a surety that this couldn't be real. It had to be some kind of cruel dream.

"I'm not much to look at in the morning."

The grin again, effortless on him, and she felt envy stir once more at his complete ease with himself.

"I wouldn't go that far," he said and touched the corner of her mouth. "But you do have a little drool action going on here."

She knocked his hand away and reached behind her for the pillow. She grabbed a handful of it and swung at him in a wide arc. He caught her arm and pushed her back down onto the bed, pinning her beneath him.

"It's okay," he said. "I like the droolers."

"I hate you."

"No you don't."

Then he was kissing her and her doubts fell away.

*** 

She decides to change tactics.

"When did you get the gun back, Miller?"

*Her gun*, she kept reminding herself. He touches the weapon, running his fingers over the cold metal barrel. For a moment, his face clears, like he's realizing what's happening, but then that empty resignation returns.

"Doesn't matter," he says.

"Charlie gave it back to you?"

He nods. She sees the man in her mind and disgust crosses her face before she can stop it. He raises his eyebrows at her, goading her.

"Charlie," she spits.

Charlie, the toad. A fat, greasy man, three times divorced, and Miller's best buddy since her affair. Charlie, who fed Miller a steady diet of misogyny and filth and leered at her with shameless hunger whenever she'd met him, the way some callous Wall Street suit might size up a hooker. It was Charlie who'd put it in Miller's head that couple's counseling was for pussies and that Evelyn could never again be trusted. Every time Miller was obstinate with

Doctor Kendra or gave some flippant answer to a probing question, she knew it was Charlie speaking through him, using her husband like some deranged mouthpiece. She felt her skin crawl at the mere mention of his name.

"You think the cops won't talk to him?" she asked. "You think they won't find out what you did here?"

He looks at her, like a tired parent going over another disappointing report card.

"You still don't get it, do you?"

He laughs then, high and unstable, and Evelyn cowers from him.

"By the time I'm done with this place, there's going to be nothing left but ashes."

\*\*\*

A month later and she was back for another Saturday at the club. No conferences this time, no excuses. She couldn't say she wandered in here on a whim anymore. She'd become something of a regular. She took a seat towards the back, nursing a glass of wine, nervously scanning the crowd, wondering how many other groupies were peppered throughout the audience. In the front row, a liquored-up bachelorette party. Tiaras and little dick straws. Homemade tee-shirts that read: *Wrecking Crew*. Miller was flirting and playing to them and they were eating it up.

There was a bright shine of jealousy, new and unwelcome in Evelyn's otherwise unruffled life. He was making her messy, that was for sure. But damned if she didn't like it.

"So, be honest, how many of you girls watch porn?" Miller asked the bachelorettes.

There were a few laughs and some hands went up. Miller rolled his eyes.

"Come on, liars! Hands up!" he teased.

The girls giggled and jostled the bride until she put her hand up in the air.

"This one," he grinned. "She's actually been in a couple, I'm pretty sure."

They cheered for her.

"I thought you looked familiar," he said and twirled his finger. "Wait, turn around so I can be sure."

That got them rolling in the aisles and Miller pressed on.

"My girlfriend has ruined porn for me," he said, looking forlorn. "One of my favorite relaxing pastimes and she totally ruined it."

Evelyn tensed in the back, not sure where this was going, feeling a strange combination of exposure and flattery.

"She comes and sits down with me one day and says: I know you watch porn when I'm not home."

He looked around, bug-eyed, first to his left, then to his right. He began to prance in one direction, then the other.

"Huh?" he asked. "What? What are you talking about, sweetheart? That's crazy talk!"

They were all grinning at him, a man caught smack in the middle of it.

"She pats my knee and says: it's okay, you're not in trouble. And I look at her, you know, is this a trap?"

He squinted, cocking his head to one side.

"She tells me: I was thinking we could watch it together. Spice things up a little…"

He opened his eyes wide and laughed.

"Jackpot!" he yelled, stamping his foot on the stage. "A girl who wants to watch porn with me? I just won the freaking kink lottery!"

They were looking at him expectantly, waiting for the punchline.

"So we're, you know, having a little sexy time and she says: hey, throw something dirty on and let's see what happens."

He reached his arm out like he was holding a remote control and punched an imaginary button.

"We're getting started and it's a schoolgirl in trouble with the teacher. And she leans over and whispers in my ear: where are her schoolbooks?"

He raised an eyebrow and looked to his right, incredulous.

"It's a porno, babe, who cares about her books? But she won't let it go. She tells me it ruins her suspension of disbelief. I tell her her suspension should have evaporated as soon as the girl started sucking on the end of her pencil, but she's stuck on the books and won't let it go."

He slapped his forehead and smiled at them.

"Okay, change of tactics. Another scene, secretary and boss: Who dresses like that for work? Okay, back to the drawing board. New scene, babysitter and dad: Where's the baby while all this is going on – that's just irresponsible parenting, no?"

They were laughing it up and Miller sensed that rising tide that carried him over the top.

"Her husband is cheating on her with her sister and she joins in? That would never happen. Next! That cleaning lady has clearly never held a mop before. Next! What's with this pool boy – she doesn't even have a pool! Next! Wait? So who's flying the goddamned plane?"

He drew breath, exasperated.

"It goes on and on like this until I'm flaccid and depressed and rethinking some major life choices. Finally we turn it off and I went to bed angry. I mean, Jesus," he said and winked out at Evelyn.

Some of the girls turned to look. She lowered her head, the blush burning her cheeks. It was time for the closer, so he set them up.

"Two weeks later, she's gone for the weekend for work and I'm thinking, it's on. Gonna reconnect with some old friends."

He strutted up and down the stage with a huge grin on his face.

"Got me a six pack, got me a box of tissues, and the big TV in the living room, let's do this!" he shouts. "So I settle in for a little bit of me-time, right?"

He clicked the imaginary button on the remote again.

"And here it is, some hottie in the bathtub when her dirty uncle catches her. And right then and there, I realize we have the same shower curtain in our house. I should be focused on the girl and the sex and the T and A and stuff, but no, I keep thinking that these porno people have the same shower curtain we do. And now I'm looking at the towels and they match the shower curtain perfectly and now I'm thinking: Where did they get those fucking towels? Ours don't match the curtain like that. Those porno people have better towels than we do!"

He sighed, trailing off, looking at them like a sad puppy.

"It's then I realized, she ruined porn for me forever."

He bowed his head and brought the microphone close.

"Incidentally, I'm still on the hunt for those towels, so if you happen to see 'em…"

The lights blinked twice in the back and he held up his arms.

"That's all the time I have folks, thank you very much!"

The crowd roared and rose to their feet. A couple of the girls rushed him onstage, eagerly stuffing dollar bills into his pants. It was the first standing ovation Evelyn had seen at the club and she swelled with unexpected pride. Miller was unfazed by all the attention. He looked out at her from the spotlight, eyes for her alone. She blew him a kiss. He reached up and caught it and she knew she'd fallen for him.

\*\*\*

Was he really going to set fire to their home? Was *that* the endgame? Again, Evelyn found herself shocked that he'd planned this out so completely – all the way through to the end, it seemed. Where had she been? How had such a change come over him and she was blind to it? Well, that was obvious, to her anyway. She'd been preoccupied. Lost in whatever transformation had come over her. And what was that, exactly? Even she was unable to see the scope of that.

"You're going to do what then? Torch our house? Destroy all our things? Our life together?"

He leaves the countertop and returns to his seat in front of her. He picks up the hammer and tosses it to the linoleum. It's a cold comfort, given the information he's shared with her, but it's a comfort nonetheless. He sits back down heavily, like he's been doing hard labor all day. He raises his head and the detached, calculated look is back. She is a specimen again.

"We're getting off topic here, I think," he says at last. "I want you to tell me why you killed Beasley."

She sighs, tired to her core. How could she possibly explain? How could she make him understand, when she herself had scarcely a clue? She decides on honesty. No point in mincing words or keeping secrets now.

"I was..." she pauses, trying to capture it as best she can. "I was trying to save him."

Miller draws back from her as if she struck him. He knew far too much about being saved from his insane mother. He remembers walking in and seeing his father on the floor all over again. He can hear the swift whistle of a knife, the wet packing sound of metal into meat. His mother pleading up at him with blood-soaked hands – *I had to save him, Milly, don't you understand?* Evelyn sees her miscalculation, but it's too late to take the words back. Distrust is dark in his eyes. He glances quickly down at the hammer, then back at her, and she feels her heartbeat quicken. His lips draw back into a snarl.

"You were trying to *save* him?"

"It's not like that," she says, reading his face. "I...I thought I could. Miller, he was hurt. I thought I could fix him."

"Explain yourself," he demands.

She had debated how long to sit with this, if she should even say anything at all. But the look on Miller's face tells her he is seconds from violence and she doesn't know what will happen then.

"Something's happening to me. I don't understand it or why it's happening to me, but it's big. I don't know how to control it yet," she says, words coming out in a rush. "I'm afraid. So you need to *stop this*, right now. You need to untie me and we can talk about it. But this? It's dangerous for me. For us. I can feel it starting again. If you try to hurt me, I don't know what will happen."

He squints at her, like she's putting him on, and settles back in his chair. He looks like a cop who's caught a perp in a lie and is sitting back to enjoy the show.

"Miller," she says, deadly serious. "I'm afraid I could hurt you."

He laughs, devoid of humor.

"I think," he says. "that we're way past that."

\*\*\*

Miller was thronged by admirers, all vying for his attention. Even Max, the owner of the club, had come out to personally congratulate him on his set. Evelyn also saw a tall man in a sharp suit slip Miller a business card and pat him on the back. She stood at the outset of the group, feeling painfully like she didn't belong, but refusing to let herself jam in with the rest of the groupies. Someone in the crowd shouted for shots and a cheer went up. The bartender laid out a set of shot glasses and proceeded to top them off with amber liquid. The glasses were passed around and Evelyn heard Max's voice boom.

"To Miller!" he shouted. "You are one funny bastard."

Bottoms up, raucous whistles and congratulations. She felt like she shouldn't be there, like she was the dorky girl who was only invited to the party because she'd be sober enough to drive her cool friends home at the end of the night. The anxiety was maddening and she debated leaving altogether when his eyes found her. He smiled at her, a real smile, not the plastic one he used to woo the crowd. He beckoned her into the circle. The crowd turned to look at her and she knew if she didn't put one foot in front of the other, she'd flee the scene.

"Yes," he said, nodding to his followers. "Make room, please."

They parted and let her pass into the inner sanctum. Miller held out his hand to her and she was grateful for it. She found it and he took it surely, rising to meet her. He turned to face the club owner.

Max was a bullish hulk of a man with a barrel chest and huge ham hands. He wore a faded leather jacket and an old tweed flat cap. He had massive diamond studs in each of his cauliflower ears.

"Max, there's someone I want you to meet."

He looked like a retired boxer and, if Miller hadn't had her hand, she would never have had the courage to meet his eyes.

"Who's this little lady?" he asked in a thick Irish cockney.

"Max, this is my girl, Evelyn."

She held out her hand politely, fearful of it being swallowed by his calloused bear paws. He reached for her, dwarfing her hand in his, and shook. He was gentler than she expected and fixed her with a boyish wink.

"We're family here, Evelyn," he said. "Welcome."

She felt dizzy, unsure if it was the third glass of wine or the gentle giant's monstrous kindness. Miller, seeming to read her mind, put a steadying hand on the small of her back. She looked at him.

"Your girl, huh?" she teased.

He grinned at her sheepishly. *Well?* She touched his cheek, fingertips tracing the line of his jaw, and nodded. The crowd roared their assent. Then someone shouted: "Kiss her!" And Miller, the consummate performer, leaned in to oblige them. There was more shouting, but Evelyn no longer heard it. All she heard was a single voice in the crowd.

*This is my girl.*

# 5

THREE DAYS AFTER the incident in the bathroom, Evelyn was managing a very different crisis at work. Her caterer had dropped out on her at the last minute and she was scrambling to fill chafing dishes with something edible before the first of the guests wandered in. It was a corporate gig, a shiny shindig with goodie bags and a premium bar. Corporate events were the easiest to manage as far at Evelyn was concerned – keep the liquor flowing and the nights pretty much ran themselves. But good booze or no, everyone screamed for carbs sooner or later.

She was explaining the situation to the contact on the phone. She exuded cool. She was on top of things. These things sometimes happen. Nothing over-the-top. No ass-kissing. The suits liked professionalism when things got hot under the collar. And options. She could call an Italian kitchen for pasta and sauces. Maybe an Asian infusion as a nod to the higher ups? Maybe just pub food so the callous-free, hardworking hands of the computer cowboys could unwind after a day of wrangling code? She already had the Asian dishes in the works with a chef who owed her a favor, but offering up options bolstered the egos of contacts who appreciated the luxury of choice.

It was a classy affair? Of course. Then the Asian infusion cuisine was her professional recommendation. Play to your audience, this was one of her first lessons in the service industry as a young caterer fresh out of college. If this were a bride on the other end? Ass-kissing like her life depended on it. A school? The complete opposite. School's could barely organize bake sales and begged for constant hand-holding. You had to whip schools in line with the stick rather than the carrot right out of the gate.

She sensed the contact relaxing and ended the call. One hour to showtime. She got back on the phone to give the Asian place the go-ahead. The bar was assembling, coming in one crate at a time. The bartenders were dawdling outside in the chill, smoking cigarettes. The five-piece orchestra was tuning up and a blonde woman with a cloud of Chanel was carefully placing centerpieces and name tags out onto the tables. A team was setting up heaters at the corner of the big tent to keep the chill at bay.

It had a hum to it, like the precision innards of a watch. People moving in concert, synchrony, previously disparate elements coming together around the gravity of the event. She loved to watch it take shape. This morning, this was an unimpressive field behind a park and now it was transforming, by precious inches, into a ballroom for a black-tie evening. No matter how many times she'd done this, Evelyn relished seeing a blank canvas fill with color. Planning it all didn't appeal to her; she found that the most stressful part of the job. It was keeping the plates spinning that made her come alive. In her mind, equilibrium was never a static process, though it may appear that way to the uninitiated – equilibrium was the sum of hundreds of minute changes and tweaks, a constant shifting of the feet to maintain balance.

Her job had changed greatly since her accident. It was more sedentary, easier than long hours on her feet, and nights like this where she was called out to an event were rare. But as much as her leg howled after she ran events, she missed the thrill of the floor. She had been accused many times of being cold – too serious – even by her husband. But she knew joy there, secret as it may be to those around her. In the orderly march of creating spectacles, Evelyn imagined she could command armies, even that she had a dim, primal predilection for war.

Her phone buzzed in her hand. She looked down: Miller calling. A terrible picture of him holding Beasley with that lopsided grin of his that said, *Trust me, babe, I got this.* It was his ritual, to call and wish her luck before the big events. Sometimes it was welcome, sometimes she'd even broken down crying to him from some sullen bathroom stall far away from her troops. But lately it had grown annoying, Miller poking his fat nose into her business, checking up on her – a helicopter husband. She stared down at the phone, resentment steadily ratcheting up to anger in her mind. She debated ignoring him. She could say she was busy, but if she didn't call him back, he'd sulk. She took a deep breath, forced herself to smile, and answered his call.

"Hi honey."

It was too sweet, just on the edge of sarcasm. She hated herself for handling him like she would any other client. She hated him more for forcing her to handle him.

"How's it looking out there today, Commander?"

Easy-going, Miller. A calming man for trying times. But she knew better by now. No matter how he appeared, her husband was always trembling on the inside. Just behind and beneath his cavalier surface was a threatening maw of uncertainty that enraged her. It was why he always threw his performances when he knew there were scouts in the audience. It's why he always clammed up when there was a fight. It's why she cheated on him. Nothing was definitive. Miller never pounced.

"It's a mess today." She paused. "This really isn't a good time."

She could feel him wilt on the other end of the phone.

"Oh…I…"

Her grip on the phone tightened. The wounded puppy. Here he was serving the ball back to her. As if she didn't have enough to do already? Now she had to coddle him and protect his increasingly delicate ego. And was there guilt there, sticking to his words like syrup? Still? She had the affair and he feels guilty about it. But that was the trick, wasn't it? His guilt only made her look like more of a bitch. He'd probably let her get away with it again, standing beside her with a lonesome smile on his face, like some politician's ditzy wife.

"Miller," she snapped. "You need to get over it."

Puzzlement on the other end of the phone.

"Lyn, what are you-"

She heard a violin come in from the orchestra. She knew a flute would follow. She turned to glance at the bar, knowing the shaky tower of wine boxes would, destroying at least a case of White Star. She felt her head jerk to the far corner of the tent. The heater had a busted coil, something had happened during transport, but there was a spare in the area – it wouldn't be a problem. The singer was stuck in traffic and the lady with the cloud of Chanel was short three centerpieces. The weather would be clear and cool and the food would arrive stylishly late.

She felt it happening around her. She was caught up in the overwhelming feeling of moving forward. All that was happening, that would happen, was somehow already finished. She could only march forward, taking her place in the procession. There was no going back. Even now, the present was erasing the past as neatly as words off a whiteboard. She could no more stop the words coming out of her mouth than she could stop the evening from happening.

"My affair. The accident. You need to get over it. We've talked it all out in therapy, and I'm done being the Jezebel. So divorce me, or move on. But I won't do this anymore."

She saw the box of champagne at the top of the pile waver, saw the corner of the box beneath it buckle with the weight above, and the top box began to slide. The crash would end the call, she had never been more certain about anything in her life.

"I have to go," she said, eyes fixated on the sliding box. "Something's happening. But Miller?"

Silence on the other end, then a wounded, "Yes."

"Please stop calling me at work."

The champagne was plummeting, turning over in space. Evelyn ended the call. The rest of the night was flawless.

***

She returned home to an empty bed. Miller was on the couch, his form of silent protest. In the fallout after the affair, they slept apart to keep from killing each other. But over the last few months, whenever Miller felt persecuted, he'd take Beasley and they'd retreat to the living room couch. It was fine with her. One of the things she discovered about marriage that she hated was sharing a bed with a sweating, snoring man-child with a propensity for kicking her in the shins when he had bad dreams. Having the big bed to herself wasn't just a luxury, it was a victory.

She slipped off her heels and sprawled out on her back on top of the comforter, sighing with exhaustion. Her leg ached. She wanted to get out of her skirt and blouse and hose and she wanted to scrub her makeup off with hot soapy water and put on her comfy clothes. She was debating a bath, but couldn't move. Despite being tired, she had to admit there was hesitation underneath. She was avoiding the bathroom. It wasn't fear exactly. If she were honest with herself, she was trying to quell a curiosity that she was certain was dangerous somehow. She wanted to know what happened in there, even wanted to know more, but intuition told her with sickening certainty that if she indulged that curiosity, she wouldn't be able to go back.

"Back to what?" she asked.

As she thought about it, sleep took her. It was dreamless and restful and when she woke, the light of day made all her late night worries seem foolish.

\*\*\*

The next morning in the bathroom, unremarkable once more, she urinated and washed her hands. Reaching for the taps on the tub to draw a shower, she saw a black speck out of the corner of her eye. She felt herself jerk involuntarily. Her hand sprang up to protect her face. Creeping things were tolerated in Evelyn's life, but if they surprised her, her responses were swift and merciless.

She swatted at the shower curtain and stamped her feet, eager to shoo it down the drain, whatever it was. She didn't care about species or identification. It was horrible and must be banished. When the black speck didn't move, she felt the tight bundle of gooseflesh at the back of her neck release. This was now merely a disposal operation.

She wadded toilet paper and leaned over the tub to scoop up the intruder. A silver glow caught her eye and she stopped. She dropped to her knees and stooped over the lip of the tub. In the tub was a dead spider holding a small pearl as if he'd captured it and died defending it. She waved an edge of the toilet paper at the pair to try and shake the carcass loose, but the creature held fast.

"You're going to make me go get a pencil, aren't you?"

No response was forthcoming. She slapped her hands on her thighs and groaned as she rose.

"Okay."

Rummaging through the utility drawer, she tried to place where she could have lost a pearl. Her modest collection of "good jewelry" lived mostly in her closet with a couple of defining pieces that she'd "loan" to herself for special occasions. She hadn't worn pearls in years-

*It's not yours.*

The thought stopped her cold and she barely noticed when a plastic clicker pencil seemingly leaped into her frozen hand. She had an image of Miller, sprawled out on the couch with the dog watching Late Night. He'd be waiting her out, wishing her to sleep so he could jerk off to porn. He'd then spend the rest of the night no doubt filling Beasley's head with fiercely whispered stories of what a bitch she was. She knew he was unhappy. She understood, more and more clearly, that they were not okay. But cheat? Would he?

*It's not yours.*

Did he?

She made a fist, clenching the pencil tightly. The impulse was more to strengthen her resolve, but once she felt the smooth unyielding plastic push against the skin of her palm, she wanted to stab something. In fact, she felt great about it. She stalked back into the bathroom, forcing herself to maintain control. Was it here?

"Did you fuck her here?"

She glared murder at the shower curtain, felt the pencil-wielding hand twitch. She had to bite the inside of her lip to keep it together. And then, fury. She tore at the shower curtain, cursing, and ripped it from its moorings, plastic rings clattering across the bathroom floor. She went to work on the liner and by the time her tirade subsided, she was breathing hard. She stared up at the light socket in the ceiling. It still remained burned out and broken. The bathroom was trashed.

Recovering her senses, Evelyn approached the naked tub. At the bottom of the basin, the spider still clutched the pearl, untouched by the melee above. She fell to her knees and poked at its legs with the pencil. Its death clutch was unaffected by her prodding. She shrieked and threw the pencil into the hallway. Her emotions surprised her, rippled through her, made her whole body shake. Tears were hot in her eyes, but she fought them back. She was dizzy. Then, like the sudden halt of wind over a lake, she was exhausted. She deflated, using the rail of the tub to collapse. She peered down, demoralized, at the dead pirate, daring her from beyond the grave to take his treasure. She frowned at it.

"Why can't you just let go?"

Like a lever or a hydraulic arm, there was a release, as if a trap was sprung. The spider's legs fell stiffly open and the pearl popped out of its clutches, hitting the porcelain with a sharp snap. Evelyn was completely entranced until the pearl began to roll towards the drain. She snatched for it, but it slipped down the hole and out of sight. She felt unsteady. The pressure of her own heartbeat thudded at her ears. She returned her attention to the spider.

It lay motionless, legs outstretched, reaching up to her. It was comical in a way, like the creature had died being tickled. But Evelyn felt a sense of opening doorways and a chill settled into the small of her back. She felt her mouth open and words forming at the base of her throat. Like watching herself drown, she was powerless to intervene. She saw, screaming and irretrievable, what was going to come next.

"Get up."

As if it had been shocked, the spider jumped upward and canted to the left. Its legs twitched, spasming as if fending off an attacker. She put a hand over her mouth and rose fast, knees popping. Swaying drunkenly, the spider tried to rouse itself. One of its legs hung at an awkward angle, shuddering, defiantly uncooperative with the others. She swore she could feel eight eyes staring up at her, sickly adoring. Awaiting instructions. It was wrong. All of the trembling thing was wrong. She felt a scream rising.

"Be dead," she begged.

The spider froze and keeled over like an outlaw shot down in a spaghetti Western. There was a seductive moment where laughter bubbled up in her, the ripcord for hysteria. Then she fainted.

\*\*\*

The shadows were longer when Evelyn came to. She sat up with a start, brushing off invisible spiders with a cry. She gasped, with a feeling like she was suddenly falling. She rose slowly and chanced a quick glance into the tub, holding her breath. The spider, now quite dead, remained keeled over like some makeshift bandit shot dead in an alley behind the saloon.

*Am I going crazy?*

In seeming answer to her question, her belly rumbled loudly. She touched it gently, frowning. It shook under her fingertips. She'd rocketed past hungry and into ravenous. She felt the overpowering need to stuff herself, as urgent and primal as any toilet need. She surveyed the bathroom, noted the shredded shower curtain and the hooks splashed across the floor like confetti. She could clean it up before Miller got home from work. Just like the light. He never came into this bathroom anymore anyway. She could probably just shut the door and no one would be the wiser. All this could wait. Right now, she must eat.

She half-staggered, half-trotted to the kitchen. She threw open the big metal doors of the fridge and stared inside with greedy eyes. A plate of lasagna and a tray of cold cuts jumped out at her. She took them out and placed them on the kitchen island with delight. She took out yogurt, a hunk of cheese, some Chinese take-out leftovers, and a quart of milk. Hunting for a fork, she freed a jar of peanut butter and a rolled up bag of Oreos from the cupboard to add to her pile. She leaned over the stash of food on the island, trying to determine how many things she could stuff into her mouth at once. Her stomach growled again, loudly, and she fell upon the food like a starved animal.

Beasley, attracted by the smells in the kitchen, walked in on Evelyn with her face inches from her collection, shoveling food into her mouth like someone who hadn't taken a meal in weeks. He paused, head cocked, watching this strange new behavior with a mix of excitement and trepidation. He whined softly at her, trying to lead this situation into treats if possible.

"Beasley!" she called through a mouthful.

He barked and ran to her, pawing at her legs, staring up at her with open delight.

"Hi baby!" she said and held up a piece of turkey to him. "You want?"

He barked again, his pawing more urgent.

"Sit."

He ignored her, whining for the dangling piece of meat. She made a mock stern face and scolded him, but with all the food and his mother obviously deranged, Beasley was overstimulated. He looked at her and barked loudly. She glanced at the mass on the kitchen island. She shrugged and tossed the turkey to the dog. As he snapped it up, she collected as much food as she could wrap her arms around and settled onto the floor beside him. He snuffed appreciation at her, sucking down the last of the meat, tongue lapping at the juices on his face. She forked a huge chunk of lasagna into her mouth and snuffed back at him.

First kill promptly defeated, Beasley surveyed the territory proudly. His nose twitched, poring over new scents. He was drawn to the Styrofoam box near the corner of the island. He edged nearer to it and paused, looking up to his master for permission. Evelyn nodded at him, lasagna abandoned in favor of Oreos and milk from the carton.

"Go nuts," she said.

The dog hesitated. Surely she wouldn't really allow this. But the smells were too enticing and he pounced. The two ate until they were stuffed. Bellies distended, they lay panting side-by-side on the kitchen floor, staring up at the ceiling as if they'd never seen it before.

\*\*\*

Miller didn't come home until after midnight. A set at the club and a couple drinks. Or a nightcap somewhere? Maybe more? Beasley stirred at her feet, barked softly at her, and left the room. He'd spend the night with Miller now, a child of divorce. The Chinese food had done nothing good to his insides and he'd been ripping punishing farts all night. She lit candles and incense, but these farts hung in the air with a force all their own.

*Poor Miller.*

She heard him greet Beasley, the welcoming barks, some roughhousing on the couch. The television came on and she heard Miller dump his gear and hang his jacket in the hall closet. The couch creaked and he settled in. He didn't come to check on her. This wasn't a first, but she felt the fresh sting of it tonight. She debated her next move. Then she heard Miller first gasp and then groan.

"Beasley, Jesus."

Laughter overcame her and she had to force a hand up to cover her mouth.

"Oh my God, dog."

She heard him shout and it only fueled the laughter. Her sides were shaking, hand clamped tightly over her face, tears streaming down her cheeks. Now he was spraying Febreze like he was gassing roaches and her belly heaved. She rolled on the bed, trying to shake free of the hilarity. Any minute now, he'd come barreling down the hallway to rouse her and she would laugh in his face, she knew it. And would that be so bad? Maybe she could talk to him about it all now, while they were both bright with the joke and feeling open?

But something kept her still in the bed, stifling laughter from her inside joke. She fell asleep chuckling to herself and dreamed that night of a legion of a thousand spiders dancing to the wagging of her finger.

# 6

SHE WATCHES HIM pace back and forth in front of her. The sound of his shoes is heavy on the linoleum. Her fear has subsided and she is regaining composure. She remains unnerved by the gun and the explosive tension in Miller's face. His sandy hair, a trademark mess, has gone beyond, into dishevelment. His face, with an easy notch in the left cheek for his lopsided grin, has drawn into a grimace of strain and distrust. His big brown eyes, her favorite feature of his, are now huge, darting around the room, seemingly unable to alight on any one place. He is courting hysteria.

He'd grown, she'd give him that. He is more alert, more in command, driven in a way she always hoped of him. And what is that? A stirring of pride in that for her? Shouldn't there be? She made him this way – she was responsible. The cost was his smile, so be it. She tries to pity his harrowed face, but the anger remains, brightly burning. She thinks of pearls and blinks back fire.

How hard would it be to melt apart the tape with her mind, call the hammer to her hand, and bury the claw end of it deep into the soft place at the corner of Miller's jaw? She blinks back violence. But didn't she deserve this, just a little bit, for shutting him out? Forcing him from her kindness? Again? She blinks back guilt.

Resentment floods her veins and she has to close her eyes. In the dark stillness behind them, she understands she is in control. She's responsible for both of them now. At his current trajectory, Miller was set to crash and burn pretty soon. He didn't know what she did and he was too erratic to reason down. One way or another, she needed to bridge the divide with him. Miller had to be on her team.

When she opens her eyes, he's staring at her. Some of the coldness has left him. There is also a faint hint of wonder in his gaze, enough to give Evelyn faith that something of the man she loves remains. She decides to give him what he wants. She tells him what she remembers of the day.

"It was Noah," she says.

He blinks at her.

"What the hell are you talking about?" he asks. "What about him?"

"He hit Beasley. He backed over him."

Miller winces and puts a hand over his eyes. Noah was grudgingly accepted into the end of their little street. He rarely left his house and then, for weeks at a time. He wore the same wool hat, independent of the weather, and he always smelled like weed. But aside from some barbecues with colorful characters and some girls in and out, he was relatively quiet. He put out his trash, he paid his bills, and blended in. Evelyn disliked him openly, but Miller tolerated his seemingly endless festival stories for a couple of joints every now and again. Beasley adored him.

Roaming largely unchecked during his out periods, Beasley would invariably wind up at Noah's house, often for hours at a time. He liked to seek shade in the hotter months under the trunk of the kid's old Subaru. Evelyn had made Noah promise he'd check under the car for Beasley when he left, and he'd held up his hand and solemnly agreed, but she saw the smirk on his face and knew he didn't hear her.

*He's going to kill him dead one day, Miller. Are you listening to me?*

He was listening now.

***

Weeks ago, when she was still trying, she'd taken Beasley out on a leash in the mornings. Lately she'd been preoccupied with more metaphysical demands and simply opened the back door for him when she woke and called him back home for lunch. Their cul-de-sac was safe from traffic and there was a hole between the fences just big enough for him to wiggle through and emerge into a world of incredible new smells. Beasley feared big trucks and barked furiously at UPS when they lumbered down into their nook. Evelyn knew he'd steer clear of them.

To his credit, the dog was a savvy mayor of the cul-de-sac. After making heated eyes with the cat in the window next door, he'd scooch down the alley between the houses to the recycle bins. A bark or two to the Labrador across the street and he'd cross the yard, perhaps at haste, to avoid the too-hard patting of the little girl two houses down. A hop off the curb and into the street, like he owned the block, and then up Noah's drive.

He'd stop to sniff the tires of the battered Subaru or roll underneath it like a pig in mud. Contented that his spot remained uncontested, he'd saunter up to the side door and scratch and whine until his idol either let him in or ignored him. If Noah didn't answer, Beasley would circle the house a couple times and then settle into his spot under the car to wait. He would chomp at bugs or chase birds, but eventually his head would grow heavy and he'd doze.

Evelyn had stopped going to work at this point. Miller didn't know, and had been keeping odd hours himself – she was almost caught at home a couple times. There were going to be questions at the end of the month when the bills came due, but she didn't think it would be much longer anyway. Whatever seemed to he be happening to her was accelerating. She'd graduated from spiders to flies on the windowsill, then a field mouse, and just yesterday a fat robin that had flown into the big bay window in the living room and snapped its neck.

She could have stubbornly insisted that the insects and the mouse had all been stunned somehow, not truly dead. But the robin had startled her – the sound of it – like someone had thrown a rock at their window. She'd crept outside with a wad of paper towels, feeling like whatever she was doing was perverse, somehow wrong. She tried to shake it off, but her eyes darted furtively from house-to-house. Who was watching her right now? She looked down at the bird. Its neck hung at an angle that refuted any possibility of life. She frowned at it, amazed at her apprehension to touch the dead thing, yet somehow calm and accepting of her ability to re-animate it.

*Not going to work through the towels though is it? You have to touch it.*

She hadn't touched the spider, nor had she touched the flies. But she sensed, deeply and surely within herself, that with a more complex organism, touch was required. How she knew this, she couldn't fathom, but she was as sure of it as she was her name and address. It had been easier with the mouse. Beasley had practically tossed it into her lap before she realized what it was. She shrieked and cupped her hands to scoop the mouse off her lap. For a moment she felt stiffness in the soft bristles and tiny bones underneath and then…what? A shifting. And then? Abracadabra? The mouse had come alive in mid-air and hit the ground running, bolting for the nearest hidey-hole while Beasley barked at it in surprise and alarm.

The bird was wild. God only knew what kind of diseases it carried. She looked around. It was the first warm day they'd had in a while. She could hear other birds and the chorus of insects. In the distance, someone had fired up a mower. It was late morning, just before lunch, and here she was in a heavy coat, thick glasses, and a scarf wrapped around her head like a hijab. Light sensitivity was one of the side-effects of her newfound powers, apparently. She could imagine how she must look standing over this dead animal in the middle of the day.

*You have to touch it.*

"Here goes," she sighed.

She knelt down, tucking the wad of towels under her knee. She peered down to study the bird. The bright fullness of its breast and the sable shimmer of its wings drew her closer. She brought her hands under it gently and lifted the robin as if she were scooping up water from a lake. She closed her eyes and felt something stir in the most primal parts of her brain. She felt a tickle, then an itch at her shoulder blades. The itch became a burn and just when she thought she couldn't take it anymore, the feeling burst into feathers and the sudden beating of wings. She knew at once what it was to fly, to surge and soar with wind as thick as ocean waves under the sturdy flap of wings. With a delirious exhale she threw up her hands and opened them. The bird leapt from her palm with a loud cry and disappeared into the treeline.

***

After the incident with the robin, wine during the day followed, and that kept her fairly even for a few weeks. She even made a few amorous advances at Miller that weren't wholly shot down. A bit of play between them returned. But she'd grown odd. She could sense it and could see the questions piling up in Miller's silences. She'd wear leggings and an old sweatshirt, unwashed hair stuffed under a ball cap, and drive to farther and farther liquor stores. She'd pretend to peruse, but was instead hunting for the biggest bang for her buck. *Throwing a party,* she'd say, but a good look behind those dark glasses brought all that into question. *Fuck you,* she'd think, *at least I'm not paying in stolen change like a drunk in the street.* Meanwhile, her savings dwindled and she found herself making increasingly elaborate excuses so she could remain at home. After a while, the clank of new bottles in the car while she drove became an irritant akin to a nest of angry wasps.

She was a glass into her second bottle the day Beasley got hit. She was lounging on the couch, listening to the breeze through the half open windows. Her attention was divided between *Ellen* and trying to levitate a pen from the utility drawer. She'd managed a paper clip, barely, and anything larger escaped her. She'd spent hours on the Internet, researching things like psychokinesis and qi, but the rabbit hole of fringe only frightened her. She stuck to trying to develop what she had. During these attempts, her head filled with running equations and something about vectors and scaling and the irrelevance of size. She didn't understand any of it, and for the duration of her experiments, the flow was constant. The TV helped to drown a bit of that out.

She heard the car start up, but didn't register anything beyond the taunting stillness of the black and white Bic pen on the coffee table. Then there was a thump, a squeal, a horrible slushing sound, and the trumpet of brakes. She heard a car door, quick steps, whining, and Noah's low, heartbroken tones. Her front door opened and she walked out into the drive without remembering how she'd gotten there. She felt herself walking out into the cul-de-sac, one foot in front of the other. When did she put her sneakers on? It didn't matter.

There was a gray lump at the base of Noah's rear tire. As she approached, it kicked softly, trying to right itself. Her vision blurred, whether from tears or dread, she could not say. She felt herself stagger and then Noah was at her side, taking her at the elbow, far stronger than he had always appeared to her. He was saying something, it had the tone of apology, but she couldn't understand the words. She felt herself nodding absently, vision narrowing to a tight cone over Beasley.

Her knees unhinged and she sank to meet him. She cradled his skull and he kissed her hand weakly. Head undamaged, that was a good place to start. She pored over him, trying to assess the worst of it. Beasley's body caved horribly inward just below his ribs. Evelyn could smell shit and knew his guts had burst. She couldn't tell if his spine was crushed and some Nurse Nancy was yelling at her in her head that to move someone after an accident will surely kill them.

"Shut up," she snarled at the voice in her head.

Noah drew back, certain she was speaking to him. She scooped Beasley up into her arms in one motion and began rushing him back towards the house. She was covered in blood by the time she reached the door and Noah was yelling after her.

"Don't you want to go to the vet?"

"I'm the vet now," she said and kicked the door open with a grunt.

She raced upstairs and heaved Beasley into the tub. He looked up at her, panting in quick bursts like a bellows. He whined, pain bright on his face. He wagged his front legs at her; there was no movement of any kind below the waist.

"Hang in there, big guy," she pleaded with him. "Mama's gonna fix you."

She was deliberating fearfully in her head all the ways in which a dog was not a bird, from spirit to anatomy. And what would happen with a creature that was still technically alive? All the others had been dead; she accepted that now. What if she somehow made it worse? Tears were close and she knew that to surrender to them would destroy any last chance Beasley may have had. She choked down a sob and forced herself to reach down and put her hands on the dog's feverish and horribly misshapen sides. She closed her eyes. Someone was telling her what happened.

*-spleen ruptured, no salvage. Stomach, small intestines, crush trauma. Spinal damage. Pelvic damage. Broken rib entering right lung. Critical injuries. Mesh team dispatched to spine. Bone gel team is on site. Right lung re-pressurization beginning now. And you. Hey you-*

It was many voices at once, a flowing dialogue, as if she were listening to an ER in real time in her head. She shook herself back to the present and chanced a look at Beasley. His eyes were mad with fright and pain. They met hers, begging.

"You're doing good, Beasley."

His tongue lolled, a bloody froth had gathered at the corners of his jowls. He shook his head roughly twice, seeming to refute her. Beasley was never going to be good again. She squeezed her eyes shut.

*-Yes you. A voice singled her out. She felt intention reach towards her through the chaos of chatter in her mind. The injuries are dire, but engineering has erected a scaffold and believes the animal can be saved. A genome template can be indexed to weave new systems. Stem cells are being seeded as we speak. We need-*

She heard a frustrated clicking in her mind. It reminded her of a stuck gear. She became aware that it was the owner of this voice, this entity, who was trying to find words to convey vital concepts to her limited and primitive mind.

*-a spark.* There was an odd mutual realization and agreement between the two of them that they understood each other. *Concentrate and imagine setting a blaze with a spark. If it helps, imagine you are holding-*

The clicking. There was an insectile quality to it, something so utterly foreign, it humbled her.

*-a sun.*

She pressed into Beasley's broken sides, gathering her forces. She breathed in and imagined hot embers packing in tightly around her hands and fingers like gloves. She forced air out in a rush and imagined the embers erupting into flames that licked healing fire deep into the dog's wounds. A protective part of her was aware she was taking orders from a voice in her head, but she was reckless. Past feeling silly or self-conscious, she treated her visualization with deadly severity, seeing rich cryptic shadows in the burning cores of her hands. Beasley shuddered. Was it working?

Her hands were hot. She was sweating. It had gathered under her breasts and at the small of her back. Between her palms, she imagined a microscopic army of engineers or astronauts or whatever they were, rebuilding Beasley cell-by-cell. She saw planking and scaffolding like bridge construction. She could hear a rhythmic clicking, tiny links weaving together into something larger, tissue knitting itself back together. Pieces of ruptured organs reached outward, puttylike, questing, searching for reconnection. Nerve fibers, thin and wispy like cornsilk, outstretched and entwined with others, reaching deep and down like roots of a tree.

For a moment, she is running. She feels the breeze on her face. And the smells! Ah, what a thing to run on four legs. So fast! She is chasing butterflies, stupidly happy, while her wolf brethren and ancestors look on from the higher mountains. She understands that all dogs are the same dog. A spirit of dogs. The condensation of *dogness*. She is The Dog and The Dog loves more than anything to run free. So all dogs do the same. Beasley is the arm of a starfish.

Then, quick as it came, the moment was gone and her hands were covered in guts and blood and they burned. There was doubt, like a spike, stabbing her quickly and cleanly. She didn't belong here. This was so far removed from anything she understood, she faltered, unsure of herself, as if looking down at the world from stilts or a high ladder, terrified of falling.

*Is Beasley ever really going to run and play after this?*

She released her grip-

*-No, stop!-*

-and felt him slip loose of her. The wolf was waiting for him and they barked greeting. He woofed at her and then they were off, racing after some unseen delight. She collapsed, exhausted. After that, it was tears for a long time.

\*\*\*

When she emerged outside, Noah was waiting for her. He'd been ambling around his car, playing on his phone, trying to look busy enough to not be obvious. He approached her, shoulders stooped, a pained expression digging furrows into his face.

"I'm so sorry. I swear I didn't see him."

She eyed him, dragging the moment out, relishing his discomfort perhaps a little too much.

"You got a cigarette?"

He inflated a bit and smiled at her. It was genuine; he could fix this in a jiffy. He dug into the pocket of his sweatshirt and handed her over a half-crushed pack of American Spirits. He wagged his finger.

"The lighter's inside."

She pulled one out and lit it. He stared at her, expectant. She held out the pack to him and he retrieved it from her. She exhaled and turned on him.

"Noah," she inhaled again. "I'd like to be alone if that's all right."

He nodded and turned to leave, then lingered.

"Hey-" he said.

Her glance was sharp.

"-I'll help you dig a grave."

She took a quick drag, biting back a sob.

"I'd like to help."

She dropped her head, a tight nod, and he was gone. She settled down on the rim of the curb, blood drying on both arms up to the elbow. It was deep under her fingernails and the smell of the cigarette wasn't enough to drown out the snap of copper. Her clothes were stained and her sneakers were bloody. She rocked back and forth on the curb, smoking and fondling Beasley's tags, and she didn't give a damn who saw her.

***

Miller is unfazed.

"You expect me to believe you?" He sneers at her. "Any of this fairy story?"

The cruelty is back. It twists his mouth down into unpleasant angles. His eyes, narrowed and beady like some underground dweller, fix her with fresh distaste.

"I know how it sounds," she tries. "But can't you at least..."

"What?" he snaps. "Believe in super powers and psychic surgery from voices in your head?"

"I know how it sounds," she repeats.

"It sounds like Burning Man bullshit!" he shouts. "Get a fucking *grip*, Evelyn. Will you?"

She knows why he's like this – a skeptic, a materialist – reducing everything down to atoms and constructs. She can empathize, even if she can't quite reach into where he's coming from. But she understands. If he accepts her crazy, her tenet that life is mysterious and pretty fuzzy around the edges, then he has to accept all the crazy. Ghosts, aliens, past lives, all the uncharted waters of the weird would flood across his levies and overwhelm him. It also meant the big crazy, the one waiting out each day at the Croupier Home for the Criminally Insane, could finally have its day in the clear cut, well-manicured court of his mind. But Evelyn needs him, now more than ever. She reaches out again.

"Miller," she says calmly. "Can you at least entertain the notion that it's possible?"

He stares at her. Then, like a metal shutter clanging shut: "No."

She knows then, like a thunderclap, without doubt. The only thing a materialist really appreciated in the end was proof, wasn't it? This argument was futile with words. One way or the other, she was going to have to show him.

# 7

MILLER EMPTIED HIS pockets while the guard rifled through his bag. He stopped when he came upon Miller's worn copy of *Watership Down* and nodded to him.

"One of my favorites," he said.

Miller nodded back.

"I read to her if she's out of it. If she's too out of it, I just sit and read. It's a win-win."

The guard waved him through the detector.

"I hear that."

Nothing beeped as Miller cleared the portal. The guard handed him his bag.

"I'm going to have to check it again on the way out, you understand."

He nodded. The ritual was worn down into grooves between them. The gatekeeper ritual: casual fondness for one another with deference to the formality that bound them both. And from time-to-time (like today, he hoped), some information was traded quietly. He took his bag.

"How's she looking?"

There was a shrug, then the guard made a so-so gesture with his hand. Here came the push.

"Do you think they'll let me take her outside?" A pause, then for emphasis: "It's beautiful today."

The guard looked towards the main doors, squinting at the light outside.

"I'll ask the doc for you. But she's gotta get her meds first."

Miller chanced it. "I'll get her pills." He pointed over his shoulder. "Nurses' station, right?"

The guard hesitated, caught between bending the rules and doing the kid a favor. Miller took one step in that direction, then two. He didn't know what he would do if he couldn't clear this hurdle. He hung suspended, breathless, until the older man nodded and waved him away with a brush of his hand. He turned down the hall, suppressing his excitement, painfully aware this was only the first move.

He approached the nurses' station, hitching his face up into a grin and then releasing, rehearsing what he hoped was forgettable disinterest. He rounded the corner-

*Please let it be one of the nurses I know...*

-and found himself staring up at the impassive face of the attending psychiatrist. He'd seen the woman on rounds and spoken to her once or twice, but she wasn't his mother's primary doctor and there was no rapport between them. Looking at her now, with her quizzical, birdlike stare, he doubted rapport would ever build, even under the most favorable of circumstances.

"Can I help you?"

"My mother, Gloria Coretti" he said.

"What about her?"

The stare was unnerving. He pointed self-consciously to the laminated *Visitor* badge on his lapel and thumbed behind him.

"George sent me to get her pills. We were hoping I could take her outside today."

She frowned down at him.

"It doesn't work like that. I-"

"It's turning into a beautiful day. I think it would be good for her to get out, no?"

The psychiatrist puzzled at him. Miller could see her frazzled with other duties and trying to interject bureaucracy on him. He rushed ahead.

"How is she doing, Doctor? Really?"

She clucked at him, annoyed at being put on the spot. She crossed her arms over her chest.

"She's withdrawn. Largely uncommunicative. Her overall health is declining. I think you'll have to meet with her primary to talk about arrangements down the line if she continues this progression."

"So…" Miller paused. "Let's take her outside then."

She was trained not to roll her eyes, but Miller could sense her irritation.

"Fine," she conceded. "Anything else today, Mr. Coretti?"

"The pills," he demanded, tapping his finger on the countertop for emphasis.

Her cheeks brightened. She pursed her lips and turned to a set of drawers. Her fingers flicked past names until she found what she was looking for. She dumped four pills into a white mini-cup and placed them unceremoniously on the counter in front of Miller, like a bartender serving last call.

"Tell the nurse on her ward you want to take her out. They'll get you a wheelchair. But they're probably not going to give you more than half an hour."

He nodded to her. He resisted the urge to swipe the pills into his hand and run, instead he forced himself to slowly reach for the cup, feigning the same level of interest he'd take in picking up his keys.

"Thank you, Doctor," he managed.

She nodded once and turned from him, back to her harried, birdlike existence. He moved for the elevator, already turning out the cup of pills into the pocket of his blazer. In the elevator, blissfully alone, he palmed the three orange Tic-Tacs and the Tylenol he smuggled in and dropped them into the empty cup. The doors opened. The hard part was over.

\*\*\*

He remembered quizzing the nurses weeks ago, when the idea of drugging Evelyn was still just the faintest of embers in his mind.

"What's this one that looks like a Tylenol?"

"Mood stabilizer," she said absently, scribbling in his mother's chart. "The other ones are run-of-the-mill antipsychotics."

He laughed at that, perhaps unkindly.

"Good to know my mother is just run-of-the-mill crazy then?" he asked.

She looked up from the chart, not amused. He wagged the cup at her to distract her, shaking the pills inside.

"And these orange ones?"

She held the chart against her breast and looked at him frankly.

"Thorazine," she said. "You don't want to be messing with those."

He grinned at her.

"Oh no?" he said. "Not even if it's Saturday and the wife is at her mother's?"

She looked at him like he was putting her on and laughed.

"You won't be doing much dancing with those," she said. "That dose will stop a rhino."

He nodded.

"Well, so much for my weekend plans."

She regarded him, uncertain what exactly to make of this man. Then she was off, checking on other patients. Miller gave his mother the pills and read to her a while as she grew bleary-eyed and began to drool. When she was deeply asleep, he left the hospital and drove three towns over to a public library. There he researched the effects and dosage of Thorazine on the public computers until the first skeletal shape of a plan emerged in his mind.

***

The duty nurse was there to greet him with the wheelchair when he stepped out of the elevator. The bird doctor, who he suspected found it intolerable to be treated as an underling, had certainly called it ahead. The nurse was a clean-shaven young man, fit and strong and sure of himself in a way Miller envied.

"We'll get her from the ward," he said and pointed down the hall. "You can wait by the freight elevator. You've got her pills?"

Miller nodded. The nurse pointed at the cup. "Keep an eye on her."

Miller nodded again.

"Just pay attention," he said. "We think she's been palming them."

Miller had suspected the same thing on his last visit, but said nothing.

"Anything else?" he asked.

"There will be a guard within twenty-five feet at all times."

A pause.

"She'll be in restraints."

A final nod. Acceptance. It had been harder when Miller was still a boy. The thick leather straps, the worn padding, stained with sweat and madness, it was an indignity. As he grew older, he was forced to deal with the reality that she was a murderer and a lunatic, but he never got over the offense of seeing his mother in chains.

The nurse wheeled the chair down the hall to Gloria's room. Miller took his time walking to the freight elevator. His pill switch would shortly answer the question about whether she was palming them. But there were other questions to be asked today, and while he was in no hurry to ask them, he knew he must. There was a window closing, he could feel it. By the time he reached the end of the hall, a cold sweat had broken out at the back of his neck and was reaching nervous rivulets down his back.

He felt her before he saw her. Gloria's gaze, unchanged by time, boring into the back of his neck. They wheeled her down the hall, a blanket skillfully covering her restraints. Her head was lolled to the side. Her hair hung, gray and lifeless, over her face. One eye blazed out at him. But it was neither glassy, nor dulled. It was lucid. And terrible. Cracked lips stretched over yellowing teeth in greeting. She might have them still fooled, but Miller knew his mother was stirring.

\*\*\*

He wheeled her up to a secluded set of tables and benches overlooking a duck pond at the rear of the hospital. The lactic fire in his muscles and the bright creak in his joints chimed resentment at him for being out of shape. He set the brakes on her chair and sat down beside her on one of the benches. She hadn't said much on the walk out, but when he produced the pill cup, she became interested. He tried to discern the look on her face, but could not.

"You gotta take your pills, ma."

He looked over towards their chaperone. The guard stared out impassively over the pond, seemingly paying no attention to them, but Miller knew that could be a ploy. He had to chance it, this was the best angle he could hope for. He rose and leaned over Gloria. She opened her mouth obediently. He cupped her chin in his hand and gently poured the pills into her mouth with a splash of water. Nothing spilled, he saw them go in. Now the waiting game. He crumpled the cup and walked over to throw it in the trash bin. He returned to sit beside her chair and waited.

Thirty seconds on, she turned on him. "What's the long one?"

"Tylenol," he said.

"And the orange flavor?"

"Tic-Tacs."

She frowned. "I don't know Tic-Tacs."

No, of course she didn't. In her mind they were probably *Sparks!* or Clic-Mints or some other tiny incongruence that would corroborate her story.

"How long have you been palming them, ma?"

She ignored him, smacking her lips. She brightened. "They're good."

"They know, ma."

She chanced a peek over her shoulder at the guard. He seemed to be ignoring them, but she was also suspicious. Suspicion was currency in a place like this.

"Oh?" she asked, as if they were discussing gossip at coffee.

"I know too."

"You know!" she shouted. "*You* don't know a fucking thing!"

The guard looked over to them. Miller put up his hand to give him the all clear, but they were actively being watched now.

"What are you up to?"

She smiled at him apologetically, like she'd made a social gaffe.

"I'm sorry I raised my voice at you," she said and cleared her throat. "Sometimes I get-"

"Cut the shit," he demanded.

She seemed wounded by his tone, but the drama was old hat and frankly tedious. She pouted and they sat in frustrated silence for a while. Finally Miller's urgent worry about the passage of time took over. He shook out a handful of Tic-Tacs into his hand and approached her.

"If you talk, they're yours,"

His hand hovered an inch or two from her mouth. She nodded twice. He scooped in the orange mints and paced around her chair while she savored them. She took her time on purpose, the seconds ticking past like a knife twisting in his belly. At last, she nodded for him to come over. He returned to the bench.

"I'm getting out," she whispered.

He looked at her. Her face was drawn, frown lines had etched cruel strokes that surrounded her lips. Her skin was sallow and yellowish, infected by halogen lighting and lax hygiene. The meds had made her doughy and slow. But her eyes were clear, bright, and cunning. He'd seen that look on her before, as a boy, when they were on the run, shortly after his father had been killed. *Murdered*, he corrected. It was determination, raw willpower, like clouds gathering before a downpour. She eyed his reaction carefully.

"You were hoping for dear doped up, mummy? Weren't you?" she teased. "Read me a bit about rabbits and then your conscience is clear for another month?"

He knew better than to engage, but her words stung through to the truth. He saw in her face that she spoke not entirely without kindness. He imagined that she did love him in her way, that there was a genuine maternal fondness for him, but that like everything else in her mind, it had become twisted out of all recognition. He pressed on.

"Out?"

"I don't belong here, Miller," she said. "*We* don't belong here. This isn't our world. You know that."

Was this talk of escape or something more dire? He gestured to the guard, fully appreciating for the first time the layers of protection in place to keep both sides safe.

"They're not going to let you walk out of here. Ever."

She looked at the guard wistfully and smiled to herself. There was a secret certainty, a knowing in that smile that chilled him.

"You have help."

She said nothing. And here was the second surety he wrestled with. He couldn't define how he knew, but he was positive.

"Has she been here?"

Silence. The calm gaze of a Buddha. Was there something of smugness there too? She'd been withering in here for almost 30 years, no one was going to rush secrets out of her in 30 minutes. The urge to beat or throttle her nearly overwhelmed him. He saw his own violence reflected in her almost serene contemplation of the lake below them. He felt his dishevelment, his sweating urgency. He sensed her power over him and had a paralyzing moment where he felt certain she was actually visiting *him* in the institution. Why would Evelyn ever come here again? After the last time had been so bad? Why was he so certain she'd been here? Why-

"You're going to drug her."

He tried to bull-charge past her serenity.

"Has she been here?"

She deflected his aggression easily and tutted at him.

"Why are you *stealing* from me, Miller? What's she done?"

He sighed, his whole body deflating around his bones. He turned up to face her and spit the words out as if just to speak them were agony.

"She killed the dog," he said. "I found the body. There was water in his lungs – the vet says he was drowned."

They locked eyes.

"I think she killed Dana too."

The name. At last. The name of their unborn daughter. A name strictly forbidden after the incident with the doll that drove them into Doctor Kendra's office in the first place. He had reached his breaking point. He feared he was fast approaching that point again.

"I need to know if she was here," he said. "Please, stop fucking around."

The guard was approaching them, tapping his wristwatch. Miller felt his chest tighten. The moment lengthened.

"Ma, please."

"No," she shot back. "Your wife hasn't been here."

It was convincing, but that special surety had burrowed itself so deeply into her countenance that she practically seeped with it. He knew she was lying.

# 8

"I HAVE TO use the bathroom."

There had been a time when he would have stopped everything at that statement. Not an open-door bathroom person and never remotely curious about toilet or menstrual habits, Miller had always dealt with these intrusions as discreetly as possible. If they were home, he'd retreat. If they were out, he'd hold her things and pace outside, like a lion defending his pride. But being forced to bathe and change his wife after the accident had erased much of his modesty. His personal boundaries were more fluid and he'd conditioned himself, like the new recruit bounds from his rack to the 5a.m. bugle and snaps to attention, to dumbly follow her needs like orders.

She missed the attentiveness, the deference. He was a knight on a quest in the beginning of their courtship, eager to prove himself. She punished him and he put her on a pedestal for a while. Reality had been unkind to them, to their marriage. She cheated on him to spite that deference, which had slowly dripped into obsequiousness. She wanted no pedestal, the expectations were unfair and impossible. Sometimes he'd look at her with such wonder, childlike, and she'd loathe him for it. It was weakness, she saw it clearly, but a soft part of her missed it and longed for it still.

"You're going to hold it."

This Miller was a monster. He was sweating, bulging anxiety, like a live wire. The contempt, so deep, just now coming to the surface. She never believed him capable of such distaste. It was Jekyll and Hyde and it frightened her. But worse was his grim certainty. He was like a man digging a grave, an unpleasant task, best to be dealt with head-on and solemnly. This Miller was going to get the job done.

She squirms. "I can't."

"Then go."

"You're the one who kept feeding me champagne."

He meets her eyes.

"*Right*," she snaps. "To drug me, then kidnap and promise to kill me. Don't think I don't know what you've done."

He looks at her, pleading to her, like it was all done out of necessity, but she'll have none of it.

"Don't paint me like I'm the only one over the line."

She snorts bitter laughter.

"The crazy hat seems to fit you just fine, Miller."

"Shut up."

"Though I suppose it's true, the apple does not fall far-"

The slap was swift and shocking and left her with tears at her eyes. She slumped in the chair and tasted blood at her lip. He was leaning over her, nostrils flaring, a froth of white had built up in the corners of his mouth.

"Did you really fall down the stairs, Lyn?"

She's afraid to turn her head. He smells sour and he's panting, sides heaving like a bellows.

"Or did you jump?"

She opens her mouth to speak and he shakes her roughly by the shoulders.

"I know you drowned Beasley!" he shouts, peppering her face with spittle.

"Miller," she pauses. "I-"

"I KNOW IT!" he screams.

She blinks and says nothing. He roars rage. He tosses her, almost enough to tip the chair over, and kicks the hammer into the corner of the kitchen. He sweeps all the tools and the ashtray on the counter into the sink with a furious cry. He kicks and knees at the cabinet doors under the counter until they hang askew in their frames. Finally he grabs the chair he was sitting on and hurls it through the glass doors that showcase their wedding china. There is a terrific crash and the sound of raining glass. Evelyn cringes and closes her eyes. Miller's knees unhinge and he collapses, exhausted, onto the linoleum, bracing himself against the cupboards.

The silence that follows is punctuated by straggling glass shards falling to the floor, settling pieces of China, and the creak of wounded wood. She listens to his breathing, finally slowing. Some of the tension has drained out of his face, most of the color too. His forehead is sheened with sweat and his eyes are still ringed with mania, but she can feel him, like coals of a great fire, cooling beneath her. She has glass in her hair and she can feel blood running down her cheek and leg.

"Miller?" she chances.

He looks up at her from the wreckage.

"I have to use the bathroom."

\*\*\*

He cuts the tape carefully, first freeing her arms, then her legs. She is unsteady, her legs feel rubbery, and any thought of overpowering him is abandoned when she tries to put weight on them. She has to lean against him for support, something she resents and suspects her husband resents even more. She grimaces as her legs start to wake up and pins and needles cry out from deep in the attachments of her muscles.

"I need to stop."

She braces herself against the wall in the hallway and sinks into a sitting position. She massages her legs, wincing and grinning without humor as the pins-and-needles sensation works through her. Miller watches her. She's been in the chair for hours. He can see the first pink glow of the dawn on the horizon.

She's rubbing the arches of her feet, eyes closed, rocking back and forth against the wall. She breathes into it, wiggling her toes, trying to pummel herself awake. Finally she stops and leans her head against the wall.

"Are you really going to kill us?"

Beasley would be stirring in another hour or so, whining and headbutting at their legs to be let out. And maybe another family member would be stirring, if things had gone differently? Would there be gurgles and happy nonsense-talk bubbling from the baby monitor? Would they share a cozy breakfast and bundle their little family into the SUV for a day at the park? Maybe the beach? What then? A sister perhaps? Graduations. Weddings. Grandchildren. A nursing home – capable, but tasteful. A shared burial plot. Tearful eulogies from their children after a long and nourishing lifetime, now well insulated from their grief by families of their own. He felt tears at his eyes.

"Let's go," he says, grabbing her roughly at the elbow and pulling her to her feet.

***

He flips up the lid and stands her in front of the toilet. He settles himself just beside her, leaned against the sink. He stares at her until she hikes up her dress and tugs down her panties. He hovers, expectant, his crotch hanging just in her periphery. Another time, this might invite fantasy, even play. Miller was a gentle man. He wouldn't be rough with her, throw her around. He wouldn't take her in *that* way. But she sometimes fantasized he would. Maybe this Miller would. She smiles in spite of herself.

"Well?" he demands.

"Jesus!" she slaps her thighs. "I need some space, Miller. I can't go like this."

He retreats to the edge of the tub, but no further, eyes trained on her as if she were a deadly convict. She closes her eyes, trying to concentrate, but she can hear him breathing. When she opens them, she catches him staring at the curve of her thighs. She grunts.

*Ha! Not so tough at all are you?*

Was there some satisfaction in that? Some nod to her vanity? *Kidnapped and humiliated and the girl's still got it.* She wasn't flattered, or touched. It was a colder emotion, a proud wind-chilled peak, littered with the frozen corpses of the fools who coveted her beauty and died trying to reach it. At least it told her that this Miller was still human with hot blood pumping through his veins. She had a chance with that. Her bladder lets go and she sighs, for a moment unable to concentrate on anything but the feeling of release.

Miller stares intently at the tiles on the floor and fidgets uncomfortably, willing her to finish, agonizing over what comes next. Telling himself it will be a kindness.

\*\*\*

He makes to get up, but she waves him back down.

"Truce. Please," she sighs. "A moment of peace."

He relents. She reaches for the tissue and wipes. She leans over and rises, pulling up her panties. She fixes her dress and flushes. At the sink she washes her hands and runs cold water over her face. She checks for more glass in her hair and frowns at the cut just below her right cheekbone. She sinks her face into the towel hanging on the back of the door, breathing in the last lingering scent of fabric softener. She looks at him, he's spring-loaded, like a trap. How long had it been since he'd slept? Or eaten? She felt her own belly rumble.

"Hey."

He looks up at her.

"How about a cigarette?"

She doesn't know if he'll go for it, but he actually smiles at her.

"Okay," he says.

He pulls the pack from his pocket and opens them. He extends the pack to her and she plucks one out. He lights his and passes the lighter across the gap between them. She takes it and settles down onto the floor, back against the door. She puts the cigarette between her lips and cocks her head slightly. She flicks the lighter and brings the flame up to her face. They smoke in silence for a minute or two. Evelyn twirls the lighter absently in her fingers.

"I didn't throw myself down the stairs, Miller."

He ashes into the drain, she mimics him, flicking hers into the toilet.

"And I didn't drown Beasley."

He riles himself, quick to do battle, but she shakes her head.

"I don't care what you *know*."

She lowers her voice.

"I would never do anything to hurt Beasley," she says. "Or our child."

He stares into the drain, refusing to meet her eyes.

"Miller," she coaxes, reaching out for him. "Look at me."

He snatches a quick drag from his cigarette and chances a look at her. She is open, vulnerable, almost inviting. Her legs are crossed over each other, her head laid back against the bathroom door. She reminds him of the early days of their engagement, when they would sit on the back stairs of his old apartment and smoke cigarettes after sex. He looks at her neck, her pulse beating visibly just at the bend below her jaw. Miller feels a stirring, something he thought forgotten. He roils again over what to do now. He meets her eyes.

"Something wonderful is happening to me," she says, her face breaking into a winsome smile.

He turns his lip up in disgust. "Here we go-"

She vaults forward and onto her knees. She reaches for him, grasping handfuls of his pants in her hands.

"It's true."

He reaches down to pull her off of him, faces close enough to kiss. She whispers to him, trying to speak past his frustration and distrust.

"I can show you."

He rises, she follows, hands up into the folds of his shirt.

"Let me show you."

He breaks away.

"Please."

He shakes his head miserably. "No," he says. "No more."

She breathes, looks him up and down, nodding to herself. He's about to take her arm and lead her back into the kitchen when she pushes him as hard as she can squarely in the center of the chest. He stumbles, mouthing an O of surprise. The tub's edge catches the back of his calves and gravity takes him. His arms pinwheel and he collapses with a graceless crash, head colliding into the back of the tub with a loud thud. She looks down at him, watching him for what feels like a stolen moment.

Then she turns and sprints for the gun.

# Act II

"You lock the door and throw away the key.
There's someone in my head, but it's not me."

-Pink Floyd

# 9

MILLER WAS NINE, trailing his mother down the aisle in the grocery store. He had only the vaguest notion his name and picture were all over the news and that his mother was the subject of an intense nationwide manhunt. He didn't know what state they were in – New Hampshire or Vermont – he couldn't be sure, they'd been driving for so long. He knew his father was dead, but he was too confused and frightened to grasp exactly what happened. All he knew for certain was that his mother was not at all right.

He glumly surveyed the candy-colored boxes of children's cereals as he followed her deeper into the store. The cartoon animals, lurid offers of treats and prizes, and the promise of sugar would normally be enough to launch heated negotiations for their inclusion in the shopping cart. But Gloria was running on empty. She was distracted and short-tempered and her dealings with him had been sharp and scolding, leaving no room for deviation. There would be no fun cereals for him in the near future.

She had been tempted to leave him in the car while she ran in, but she worried someone might see a child alone in a car and start getting nosy. She unearthed a battered baseball cap from the trunk of the freshly stolen car and fixed it on his head. She tucked his hair up under the brim and looked at him.

"Here," she said. "Zip up your windbreaker."

She covered her head with a scarf and dark glasses and hurried them both into the store, alert for signs of incongruity. This was the only store for provisions in town and it was a risk. They had been running low on supplies for days and she finally accepted they needed to stock up if they were to keep going. She knew others would track her credit cards if she tried to use them and her stash of cash was drying up. At a rest area off the highway, she'd switched plates with another car and stolen a woman's purse off a chair in the McDonald's. Back on the highway, safely away from the scene of the crime, she forced Miller to root through the woman's purse to sort out cash and valuables.

He knew this was wrong, all of it, but he was too dependent on her for his very survival to go against her. He had thought about running away, had even had the chance a couple of times. But each time he prepared himself, he fell again under her shadow, like a rocket unable to escape its planet's gravity. Where would he go? He had grandparents, some aunts and uncles, but how would he get to them? What would he tell them when he got there? Worse was the guilt. Under her harsh exterior, he sensed she was badly frightened and starting to lose control. He would look at her, see that she needed him, and a noble sense of loyalty would tug him endlessly back into her orbit.

Leaving the cereals behind, he followed her towards the deli and meats. She hovered over cuts of meat, adding up sums for their supplies in her head. Miller hovered near her, eager to touch her for some reason, to make contact, even if only to verify she was still there. He doubted very much if she'd be comforted by his touch, but he wanted to be close to her just the same. He sidled up alongside her, pressing into the warmth of her, hoping she might deign to put an arm around his narrow shoulders. Instead she moved away, seemingly annoyed with him.

"Mom-" he began, the need to be paid attention to outweighing his caution.

"Stop standing around," she snapped. "Go get eggs and milk and meet me back here."

"Mom," he repeated.

"Go," she said. "Now."

Dejected, he turned and left her fussing over the meats, trudging weightily down the aisle in search of the dairy coolers. He passed the big swinging double doors that led to the back stockroom of the store and saw the bright yellow markings of butter boxes coming up on his right. He leaned down, poring over the cheeses, stomach churning loudly. He wondered if he could sneak some cheese into their provisions without her noticing. The thought made him smile and he reached for a big block of Irish pub cheese.

Suddenly there was a hand over his mouth and he was being dragged back towards the big double doors. He tried to scream, but the hand was clamped down tightly. He struggled, kicking out, trying to free himself, but whoever had him was big and moving swiftly. The doors loomed ahead like jaws and he redoubled his efforts to break free.

He was certain, as if stuck in the slow molasses of a nightmare, that if taken behind those doors, monsters would devour him.

He was pushed through the opening roughly into a dimly lit stockroom. He saw light coming through the front of the coolers and sensed that world of warmth and people was slipping forever out of his reach. His captor set him down on the floor in front of two adults, a man of average height and build and a dark, petite woman with kind eyes. Both of them wore suits. The woman kneeled down to his level and smiled warmly.

"I have a boy about your age," she said. "His name is Wade. I'm Nora. Nora Alvarez. I'm an agent with the FBI. No one is going to hurt you, Miller, but you can't scream. Okay?"

He nodded. The agent pointed to his mouth and the grip over his face was released. He breathed and turned, looking up at a powerful man in jeans and a thick flannel workshirt with a gun at his hip.

"I'm Commander Clark. I'm sorry to frighten you," the man said, looking down at him somberly. "We had no other choice."

Miller felt a tickle at the back of his neck. His mother was looking for him. He was taking too long and he could feel that angry, buzzing Mom-radar pinging off the walls to locate him.

"My mom," he stammered. "She's looking for me-"

"We don't have much time," said Agent Alvarez. "I need you to tell me if you're mom is armed. Do you know?"

He thought of the lump in her purse, the way the bottom hung awkwardly from the weight of it. He hesitated, never more afraid in his life. Then he nodded.

"Dammit," said the man to Agent Alvarez's side, presumably her partner.

"We can't do it now," the Commander said.

She squeezed Miller's shoulders. Her hands were strong and steadied him.

"We're going to get you out of this, Miller, I promise. But we can't do it here. Do you understand? There are too many people, someone might get hurt."

He looked at her, expectant.

"You're staying at the Econo-Lodge up at the mountain, yes?" she asked.

He nodded.

"Room number eight?"

How did they know this? How long had they been following?

"Yes."

"Good," she said. "It's just you and your mom, right? No one else?"

He nodded again.

"Has she said anything to you about where you're going or what her plan is?"

He felt a twisting in his guts and knew he was betraying his mother just by being here, just by talking to these people. Was he a bad son? Was he the one who would be responsible for her capture in the end?

*I need you to tell me if your mom is armed?*

Or her death? He could feel himself hesitating again, aware of the clock ticking, and his mother's roving radar.

"She says we're going home tonight," he blurted, unable to stop himself. "I don't know what that means."

He was close to tears and his breath came out in quick, jagged puffs.

"I…" He fought back the tears. "I think something's wrong with her."

Agent Alvarez passed a glance to her partner that Miller couldn't decipher. She looked to the Commander.

"We can move on the motel tonight, just after dark," he said. "We need him to make an excuse to leave the room."

"Okay?" she asked.

"Okay," Miller said.

"Whatever you have to say, we don't need much time, but you have to be out of your room. You leave and head for the manager's office and don't look back. I'll be waiting for you. Do you understand?"

"Yes," he said, reeling, trying to process the new information.

"No one does anything until we see you leave safely," Commander Clark said. "This will all be over for you soon, son, I promise."

"Please," he begged. "Please don't hurt my mom."

Agent Alvarez shook him gently.

"Listen to me," she said. "We don't want anyone to get hurt. Not you or your mom. But we need you to do exactly as we tell you. Can you do that?"

His mouth trembled.

"You're being very brave," she said. "And there are a lot of people working to help you. But we need to work as a team. I need you on my team."

"Okay," he whispered.

The Commander waved his hand, spinning his index finger.

"We have to wrap this up."

The other agent moved to the coolers and peered through them out into the store.

"Coast is clear," he said.

The Commander opened the double doors for him and with one last nervous glance behind him, Miller emerged once more into the light. He blinked, terrifically tempted to just bolt screaming down the aisles, out the door, and away forever, from all the things in the world that made him feel small. He hurried, snatching up a quart of milk and a carton of eggs, cheese forgotten. He made his way back to the deli, but she wasn't there. He was about to head up to the checkout lanes to find her, when her voice leaped out from a nearby aisle. He jumped and turned to face her, furiously wishing his face into a neutral expression.

"There you are," she said. "Where have you been?"

He shrugged and held up the provisions.

"Just getting the milk and stuff," he said.

She looked at him with a mixture of incredulity and impatience. There was a mote of suspicion there, an uncertainty – something wasn't quite as it should be. But she was too tired to pursue it and they'd been in here too long. Every second that ticked by was a chance for someone to recognize them.

"Well, let's go then."

She strode ahead of him, making for the front of the store. He took one more look back to the double doors, and then followed her dutifully to the checkout.

\*\*\*

Newly alert, Miller scanned the crowd. He could feel, just as keenly as his mother's built-in radar, the presence of law enforcement. In fact, it was so palpable he was shocked that his mother couldn't feel it for herself. But then, he reasoned, she was seeing law enforcement under every rock and behind every tree – what real difference would it make in her stress level if the danger was real or perceived? He worried for them then, for her especially. He felt pressured by these feelings, hammered by them, in a way that was too big for his small set of experiences to still (if ever) fully understand. He imagined himself like a balloon, swelling fuller and fuller with air, his skin taut and thinning, pulling tighter and tighter until he must surely burst.

There was a man at the magazine rack by the entrance, flipping through a *Natural Awakenings* magazine. But his eyes were blank. He was flipping, pretending to peruse the articles, but it was clear he wasn't registering what he was seeing. Every few minutes or so, he'd look up, like he was waiting for someone and killing time. His gaze would invariably turn in their direction. One of the stockboys was a little too old and a little too hard-looking to be a small town stockboy. One of the checkout girls kept looking their way too, her lane becoming clogged with irate customers – she didn't know how to use the register.

Miller was too young to understand the concept of the cuckold, but he knew well enough what it felt like to have people talking about you behind your back. He understood the claustrophobic panic that rose when everyone else was in on the joke but you. And how would this joke end? Not with ribbing and horseplay, he was sure of it. He'd seen enough TV and movies (even the R-rated ones he wasn't allowed to watch) to know there were guns at the end of this joke. *Bang!* Surprise.

He shivered. Gloria frowned at him and pulled him closer to her.

"What's the matter with you?" she asked.

He shifted from foot-to-foot like he had to go to the bathroom. It was all becoming too much. He couldn't stand it. How could she not know? He nodded, trying to escape her scrutiny, knowing that if there was a single weak link in the FBI's plan, he was it. She'd sniff it out of him, somehow, she always did. She put a hand on his forehead under the brim of his cap. She scowled at him.

"You're all sweaty," she said, and then quickly prodded his neck, feeling for swelling. "You're not getting sick, are you?"

"I'm okay, mom," he lied. "I'm just cold."

This last part was true. An unrelenting chill had settled on him, clinging to him like he'd walked through a spider web. He missed his dad, suddenly, urgently, and realized that if (*when!*) they took his mother, he'd be all alone. *You will not cry,* he told himself, repeating the phrase with religious fervor like a catechism, though his family did not consider itself religious and he never thought of himself as particularly spiritual. He repeated his mantra over and over until they had moved through the line, paid, and were leaving through the automated doors in the front.

He risked a look back and saw the man who had been leafing through the magazines staring out after him. The man nodded once.

*Bang! Surprise.*
The chill crept deeper.

\*\*\*

"Why don't we just go," he said at last.

They'd been riding back up the mountain from the store in strained silence. He'd been sullen and preoccupied and Gloria seemed to be wrestling with her own inner turmoil. She'd tried to liven the mood between them by clicking on the radio, but after scanning a few stations, they'd come across a broadcast:

"The search continues for fugitive mother, Gloria Coretti and her kidnapped son, Miller…"

She stabbed at the button on the radio.

"Kidnapped," she spat under her breath, like a curse word.

Miller said nothing. The search was over, as far as he was concerned. The game was up, and the only one who didn't know it yet was his only true link to a world that largely overwhelmed and confused him.

"Well," she said. "You're famous, Miller. How about that?"

She laughed, but it was pained, like the wheezy chuckle of a long-time smoker. He said nothing, feeling invisible walls closing in on both of them. He watched the roads for following cars and occasionally he glanced skyward, looking for helicopters. Whatever else their pursuers might be lacking, they were good at keeping hidden.

He felt her tense next to him as they passed a state trooper hidden in a truck turnabout, trapping speeders. She took her foot off the gas and the car slowed. She put both hands on the wheel and eased past the trooper. He did not follow. She relaxed and Miller saw her mouth inch up into a self-satisfied smirk.

*She fears a single claw when the whole beast is upon her.*

The thought shocked him, so alien, so adult, so unlike the usual bevy of thoughts that crowded his young mind, jockeying for position. It was then, the new thought took root, desperately welcome, like long, swelling rains after a harsh drought. Maybe if they just kept driving, just pushed through the night and kept at it, they could escape the net and-

*And what?*

Uncertainty chewed loudly at him, but hope was louder still. It cried out to him that if he only stayed with his mother, if they only stayed together, everything would be okay.

"Go where?" she had asked.

"Canada. It's gotta be close to us, right?"

She touched his cheek. He resisted the urge to rub his cheek into her palm to absorb her warmth.

"It's cold there, kiddo," she said. "Way colder than it is here."

He was not deterred. The fact she was even playing along fueled his hope.

"What about Mexico?" he suggested.

She didn't have the heart to tell him that they'd be promptly stopped, searched, and taken into custody if they showed themselves at either border. She also knew that it was all coming to a close very soon.

"It doesn't matter anyway, honey," she said. "We're going home tonight and then this will all be over."

*This will all be over for you soon, son, I promise you.*

He put his cards on the table, sensing too that a window was closing and there was no more room for subtlety.

"What does that mean?" he asked.

"I mean our real home," she said, smiling brightly at him.

There was too much to that smile. Too many teeth, too wide, straining her face. The facsimile of mirth came across as ghastly, even unhinged. Miller was too young to understand the concept of madness, but he knew well enough what it felt like to have his reality pulled apart like taffy. Something was wrong with her. He could see it in her face and smell it in the sour reek of her sweat. She seemed to be buzzing, nearly audible, a high, manic keening that was rising in pitch with each passing hour.

"You just have to trust me, Milly," she said.

But he didn't, and under all the raw and the scared and the uncertainty, he feared this truth most of all.

\*\*\*

"Mom, can I go get a Coke out of the machine?"

She looked up at him, confused and a bit flustered. From the bathroom came the sound of running water – she was filling the tub for his bath.

"You barely touched your dinner," she chastised. "And now you want sweets?"

It was an old argument, somehow rendered absurd by what both of them sensed was coming. She looked around, that keening inside her seeming to grow louder in the quiet of the shoddy motel room.

"Your bath is ready," she said sullenly, as if this would stay him somehow.

There was urgency, a *need* for him to do as she said. He feared the sound of water now, and somehow grasped what it was she truly meant by "home". He had an image, fleeting but vivid, of her hands settling over his small chest and pushing him, gently as if he were being baptized, under the water. He suppressed a shudder and forced a grin onto his face.

"I'll get you one too," he teased.

She hesitated. The alarm clock on the end table between their beds read 7:07.

"Please," he added.

She sighed, defeated, and reached for the dwindling pile of stolen cash on the tired dinette that served as their dinner table. She peeled out two ones and slid them across the table to him.

"Okay, kid, you win."

He did his best to smile and pocketed the cash, rising from the table and eyeing the door.

"Come right back and don't talk to anyone. You got it?"

His hand hovered over the knob to the door.

"Miller?" she asked.

He turned.

"Is there anything you want to tell me?"

The moment stretched between them. He could almost hear the clacking of weapon magazines and smell the tang of gun oil outside. She looked small from here, from his perilous vantage point. She looked weak, and tired, and old. Beyond pity, he felt a tugging in his chest.

"I love you," he said, and meant it.

Her face broke into a serene smile that made his eyes water. She grew then, in beauty and presence. He chose to leave her this way, the last memory of his mother as she was, as she'd always been in his heart. His hand turned the knob. He pulled the door open and was through. He lingered on the other side, pressing his forehead deeply into the stained and peeling wood of the door. The mere inches between them felt forever impenetrable. A barrier between them would now always exist.

"I'm sorry," he whispered.

Then he turned, and ran. He bolted past the soda machines, past the main office, through the parking lot, and into the street. Even as police yelled at him to stop and the first tactical group began to stack up around number eight, he ran. His heart hammering and his breath an inferno, his muscles burning with exertion, he ran. On and on and on.

In many ways, he never stopped.

# 10

MILLER HAD GOTTEN home from work to find Evelyn in a black mood. He tried to maneuver around it, stepping around her apathy and sarcasm as an Army engineer would negotiate a minefield. But she was in one of her *I'm going to shoot any target that pops up* moods and before long, tempers flared and they were shouting at each other. He had accepted in their marriage that there would be days where he was the punching bag, and to her credit, he'd dished out some damage too in his moods. But ever since her fall, she seemed to have abandoned the gloves altogether.

Four pins in her right leg, a titanium rod and screws holding her right forearm and wrist together, two broken ribs, and one dead baby. It was a grim tally, and her recovery had been long and arduous. Her time in a wheelchair had been the hardest. She required constant attention and Miller spent most of his days hurrying her from surgeon to physical therapist to pharmacist and back again. He had to bathe her, change her, and he was baldly confronted with the intimacies of her toilet habits.

Miller believed, with some healthy sarcasm of his own, that the whole *in sickness and in health thing* was nothing more than some fluffy greeting card sentiment designed to create even more impossible expectations for the happy couple to live up to. But the reality of the situation, the real and gritty glue of it, was almost too much to bear. He hated himself for being weak, for being tired, for having days when he'd sit up at the throat of their cul-de-sac after a long day at work and debate with increasing seriousness the idea of putting the car in gear and driving West until he had chased the sun all the way down to the sea.

She clung to him, nursing from him with the wet trembling beak of a newborn bird, but she wasn't there. In the beginning, she slept for heroic stretches of 15-18 hours. He expected much of that was her body needing to mend itself. But in her waking hours, she had taken on a blank, flat aspect that was eerily reminiscent of late-stage Parkinson's. He blamed much of her dissociation on pills. Her injuries were grave and the docs had been overly generous with dispensing opiates. They made her groggy and thick like she was coming to him across an old phone line. Her speech sometimes slowed to monosyllables and the luster in her eyes dimmed. She would cry, often without any warning and sometimes without even being fully aware she was doing it. Most of the time, he'd find her just staring at the television, or sometimes at nothing at all – that always creeped him out. She wasn't watching anything, just staring wall-eyed out at the world like an empty socket.

When she began to come around, it was either in seeping, snot-caked breakdowns or intense rages that could flare up and travel in all directions like wildfires. That was the darkest period for Miller. His nerves were fried from either trying to deflect or defuse her steady but unpredictable stream of raw emotion. It was impossible to combat and interrupted every single aspect of his life, from his sleep schedule to his morning commute. He had new appreciation for soldiers who endured the chaos of guerilla warfare and he wondered, as surely as they must, how much longer he could survive it.

She still walked with a slight limp. The arm would heal fully in time, but the doctors believed the limp in her leg was permanent. Still healing, she held her arm motionless and close to her body when she walked, making her look like a speakeasy sheriff, ready to draw and bring law to the lawless. He started calling her "The Duke" behind her back. *Okay Pilgrim*, he'd say under his breath when she'd send him off on one errand or another. He wrestled with telling her, he wanted so badly to share something silly and lighthearted with her. He wasn't making fun of her or trying to diminish her agonies, he was merely trying to find some much-needed levity in what seemed to be crushing tragedy. But the minefield was always active. He must navigate carefully or risk spinning her into a tearful, hitching spiral.

That night, her limp was pronounced. This was a new thing (a dirty trick as far as Miller was concerned) she would roll out when she felt somehow outgunned or unappreciated. He couldn't outright prove she was doing it on purpose, and to accuse her would be to invite total, laser-focused destruction. But after coming home only to be soaked in her hostility again, he hated her for it. He had been tiptoeing on eggshells with her for over a year and his patience had worn taut and shiny, like the elbows of an old suit. The ice they were standing on was perilously thin and, greeting card vows or no, he was ready to stomp his foot right through it and drown them both.

"So just go then!" she shouted.

He squeezed the bridge of his nose and choked back the venom that threatened to spit out of him.

"Lyn, I just want to go do a set at the club and then I'll come right home," he said, trying to sound as reasonable as possible.

"No, it's fine," she said, matching his tone with mocking contempt. "Just leave your injured wife and go have a good time with the fellas. Who's stopping you?"

He refused to be daunted by her, trying instead to offer a generous compromise.

"Why don't you come with me then?"

The idea struck him as one of the better ones he'd had in a long time.

"Yeah," he said, trying to generate some momentum. "Come with me, Lyn. When's the last time we got out of this house and did something fun? Whaddya say?"

She snorted.

"You think I want to sit in that smoky shithole while you and the rest of those clowns laugh at each other's fart jokes?"

"We met in that shithole," he said wryly. "In case you'd forgotten."

"What does that say about me then?"

He narrowed his eyes.

"You know what, forget it," he shouted. "You want to sit here and wallow in it, go crazy, but I'm done."

She sneered at him.

"Like you've ever lost anything important."

He looked at her, stunned by the precision of her coldness – she knew just where and how to hurt him. He had never struck a woman, not once, but for the first time in his life, he ached to wipe that smug dismissal off her face with his fists. He knew if this continued any further that he'd say or do something he couldn't take back. He silently took his keys and phone off the table and brushed past her.

"Go!" she screamed. "You fucking coward!"

There was more, but he was already stomping out the door, his keys squeezed tight enough in his palm to carve deep, bloody grooves into the flesh.

***

The crowd was thin, but he didn't care. It had been fourteen months since he'd done a set and he was surprised how much he missed it. His circle of friends had dwindled since college, even more so since he got married, and the few that remained had begun to splinter off into their own lives as kids and careers moved to the forefront. This was one of the more jarring and lonely truths about getting older that weighed on Miller as things with Evelyn continued to deteriorate. The club was an oasis that he reached for and dreamed of, sometimes deliriously, in the desert of his current situation.

The club crew was small and word had gotten around pretty quickly about what had happened. He was greeted like a returning hero from the foreign shores of battle. They surrounded him with hugs, cheers, and claps on the back. Someone placed a sweating cocktail in his hand, and he was ushered up to the stage.

"Ladies and gentlemen, back from the dead and twice as ugly, please give a warm welcome to our good friend, Miller Coretti!"

He stepped up and approached the microphone, blinking under the hot lights. He was ready to spend his five minutes bashing his wife in the most colorful ways possible. He had made a promise to her, years before, when they were still dating. *Miller, promise me you'll never use our problems in one of your bits, I don't want strangers knowing our business.* Lovestruck, already socking away any extra cash he could scrape up to get his hands on a ring, he had agreed. But as he stewed in the truck on the drive over and railed at her in loud imaginary arguments, he felt sure that promise would fall by the wayside. Yet, as he reached for the microphone, he saw the blood drying and crusty on the inside of his palm. He knew then that if he started in on her, he would hammer it home, and it would be mean-spirited. Despite his frustration, he couldn't bring himself to do it.

"Okay," he said. "Raise your hands if your parents are insane."

The old standby worked just as well, he supposed. A few hands went up and there were some good-natured smiles peppered amongst the crowd.

"So my mom's crazy."

"How crazy is she?" came a shout from the bartender, winking at him.

"My mom is so crazy that when the doctors examine her they have to use a telescope."

There were a couple of chuckles. The bartender gave him the thumbs up sign and patted her heart, bowing her head to him. Miller was struck with a feeling of strangeness, a sense of dissociation, like he was watching himself speaking from far away.

"No, I'm not kidding," he said. "She killed my dad and she tried to kill me too."

An uncomfortable silence washed across the tables and Miller cleared his throat loudly.

"I mean, in her defense, I was a pretty shitty kid."

A couple of forced laughs wafted his way, but he was starting to sweat and he felt that dissociation intensify.

"I'll tell you though, you clean your fucking room spic-and-span when murder's on the table."

He forced a laugh himself, but thought it came out high and awkward. He wagged a finger at them, as if to scold them.

"I swear to Christ, if I find any more skidmarks in your Jockeys," he made a gun with his hand. "You are gonna get it, mister."

"Get off the stage!" came a slurring voice from the back row of tables.

Heckling was not uncommon, especially in amateur clubs like this one. Most of the time, you just brushed it off and took it in stride. If you were good, you shut them down fast and clean and moved right into the next bit. If you were very good, you shut them down in a way that made them respect you, or at least appreciate what you were offering. Miller was a traditionally easy-going performer and he knew his set was tanking fast, but this heckler crawled right under his skin and burrowed.

"Get off your knees, you fucking cocksucker," he snapped.

There was an unkind edge to his voice that bordered on violence and he regretted the biting nature of his remark, even as it ejected from his mouth. The heckler fell silent, but there was a stirring in the crowd now. They were starting to turn on him. He scanned the club. The bartender and his other friends were watching him with pained expressions on their faces. But there was no retreat, he was in it for the duration.

"Okay, what was I saying? Oh yeah, mom's insane," he said, trying to salvage it. "Well, I'll tell ya, it certainly makes screening out dates a lot easier when your mom's nuts."

It was unraveling. The tables had begun tuning him out, talking quietly amongst each other or choosing this point to excuse themselves to the bathroom.

"I mean, if you bring a girl to meet mom in the asylum and they get along?" he swiped across his forehead, now sheened with nervous flopsweat. "Phew! You. Are. Fucked."

It was cute joke and it should have elicited some life from them, but they had already dismissed him. Cruelty and meanness were the fastest way to lose them. If they got a whiff of that in your character, it didn't matter how funny you were, they reacted like startled animals to your voice.

"You know, they start trading recipes on how to stew a human head," he said. "They go shopping for strait jackets together."

They were gone. He was abandoned on stage. He sighed heavily into the microphone.

"I'm sorry," he said. "My wife is sick, I…I shouldn't be here."

There were murmurings in the crowd, audience members looking at him with a mixture of pity and anger.

"I…" he tried again, but there was nothing else.

The lights flashed twice in the back. They were cutting him early. He knew two minute and five minute sets like the back of his hand, and there was no way he'd run his time out. Maybe they were trying to save him from any further embarrassment. But darkly, he wondered if they were just trying to get him offstage before he made them look any worse. The host strode back out on the stage. He clutched at Miller's shoulder and gently moved to take the mike out of his hand. He had his ringmaster smile plastered on his face, but behind it, Miller could see sympathy.

"Ladies and gentlemen, please give a warm round of applause to our man, Miller!"

There was scattered polite applause from the audience, but they were eager to be done with him. Head down, defeated, Miller took his cue and slunk off the stage.

\*\*\*

His friend Charlie was waiting for him at the bar. Miller sat down heavily and the bartender slid a whiskey over to him.

"That was a fucking slaughter," he said.

Charlie tipped the rim of his glass against Miller's.

"You're rusty, don't sweat it," he said. "We all have a bad set every now and then. Happens to the best of us."

Miller nursed the drink. He knew his friend was right, but there was something else, something different about the whole evening. He couldn't put his finger on it, much less articulate it, but he felt like he was treading through the skeletal remains of a carnival after it had passed through town. There was evidence that something bright and fun and slightly surreal had stood there, maybe even mere hours before, but he had missed it. The circus had passed on without him, leaving him surrounded by ghosts, the fading smells of cotton candy and roasted peanuts, the echoes of kids laughing and screaming, discarded candy wrappers flapping in the breeze. There was a singular loneliness to it that made him feel like crying.

"Hey," Charlie said, snapping him out of his reverie. "I heard what happened with Ev. I just wanted to tell you that I'm sorry."

Miller turned to look at him. He was expecting something brassy and crass, the underbelly of Charlie's disdain for the fairer sex. But he surprised him.

"You both deserve better," he said and raised his glass. "I mean that."

Miller raised his own glass in return.

"How are you, man?" Charlie asked. "You look like shit."

Miller sighed. He raked his hand over the five-o-clock shadow on his cheek and shook his head, smiling without humor.

"Yeah, I don't know, it's just..." He looked at his friend, reaching for the word. "Tough."

Charlie nodded sagely, as if he understood everything, and encouraged Miller to continue.

"I mean, she cheats on me. Okay. No one tells you marriage is really like this, I get it. Am I a sucker for staying with her through that? Maybe, but I love her, so we make due. Then there's all this reconciliation and exchanging truths and all the rest of that love-language bullshit. Then? Preggo. Like that's going to fix everything. You know what it's like laying awake at night wondering if it's even yours?"

Charlie said nothing, but his mouth twisted into a tight grimace and Miller saw the empathy of experience in his eyes.

"But you deal, you know? The alternative is such a ballbreaker, you just don't think, you double down on her. What the fuck else can you do? She hasn't been happy for years. Fuck, maybe she's never been happy. You gush over names, you shop for stupid shit, she starts getting big. This is really happening. Then bam, she's down fifteen stairs and your kid is dead before she's born and your girl is crippled. And it's up to you to keep it together now, and somehow you do. But somehow, this is still all your fucking fault."

Miller doesn't realize he's doing it, but he's been spinning his wedding ring around his finger in anxious twists.

"I'm just done, you know?" he said, and then, as if the word defined everything in his world: "Done."

Charlie absorbed this, seemingly in deep consideration. Finally, he slugged back the last of his drink and banged on the bar with both hands – rat-a-tat-tat – like he was bopping on bongos.

"Miller, my friend," he said. "I'm gonna let you in on the secret world of broads. You ready?"

Miller doubted sincerely whether a toadish amateur comedian with three divorces under his belt who referred to women as broads had anything groundbreaking to offer him. But he realized venting to a sympathetic ear was the closest to therapeutic he'd gotten in a long time. Two more whiskeys appeared before them. Charlie waited until the bartender was out of earshot and then leaned into Miller.

"They have no idea what they fucking want half the time," he said. "And when they do, it comes from here."

He patted his heart.

"Not here."

He tapped his temple.

"You follow?"

Miller grinned at him, incredulous, like he'd trekked halfway across the globe to find the secret of life and found out it was more sit-ups or cutting out dairy.

"What the fuck does that mean, Charles?"

Charlie turned on him, a quick look of indignation flashing across his face.

"It means live your fucking life, mate," he insisted.

Miller stared at him blankly. Charlie sighed, exasperated.

"She's going to keep doing whatever she wants. No matter what you say or do, she keeps putting her own shit in front of yours and it's time for her to deal with it, not palm it off on you. Stop fixing, start living."

Miller grinned again.

"You gonna put that on a tee-shirt?"

Charlie growled.

"How about I carve it into your tombstone after she breaks your back?"

Miller waved him off.

"Easy killer, I'm just here to blow off some steam."

Charlie dismissed him, looking out over the bar, lost in his thoughts. He spoke to Miller sidelong without looking at him.

"You stayin'? I'm buyin'."

Miller shook his head.

"I told Lyn I'd come home right after my set."

Charlie turned on him and stuck a fat finger under his nose.

"This is what I'm talkin' about."

Miller put his hands up, as if to say: *What can I do? These are the rules.*

"I…" he started.

"What do you want to do?" Charlie asked. "*You*, not her."

He thought about it, more deeply than he'd thought about anything in a while. Then he smiled at Charlie conspiratorially.

"I want to keep drinking."

The finger retracted into a fist and Charlie pumped it in the air like his team had just won the championship.

"Jesus Christ!" he shouted, laughing heartily and clapping Miller on the back. "I think there's hope for you yet."

So Miller sat and they drank late into the night, and Charlie steadily filled his head with poison.

# 11

DRUNK, ITCHING FOR a fight, Miller struggled to stay in his own lane. The SUV lurched side-to-side, hugging the rumble strip, until he'd yank the wheel back, overcorrecting, and veer the truck wildly towards the median. He'd waved off offers to take him home or call him a cab and insisted he was fine to drive. He drove fast, reckless, blaring angry music, practically daring the cops to catch him in the act. Again. He'd gotten a DUI shortly after Evelyn's affair, his first, and it had been an ordeal. The sheer embarrassment of having to call his estranged wife in the middle of the night from the drunktank to bail him out swore him off drinking for a long time. Yet here he was. The sober and rational part of his mind knew one DUI was a mistake, while two was a pattern, but he was past caring.

Charlie had bolstered him with liquid courage and rants about "living life on his own terms" and he had reached out to capture and contain that feeling, like catching fireflies in a jar as a boy. But underneath, worming its way deeper into his heart, worked an irreparable loneliness. He had taken no succor at the club, despite the warm welcome and Charlie's impromptu self-help bootcamp. He had felt like a stranger there, like a has-been, returning to the site of his former glory, shocked that his legacy had faded with time. It reminded him of going back to elementary school as an adult and marveling over how tiny the desks were – how impossible it seemed that such a place was once the width and breadth of his entire experience.

With the loneliness came certainty. He had crossed through a portal now, a Rubicon (*alea iacta est!*), and through it, he was unable to return. Even if he could, like those tiny desks, nothing back there held any sway over him anymore. The trappings and comforts of his old haunts would no longer serve him. He had stepped into a wholly new territory. But where there should be a sense of growth, even of exhilaration, there was only a sad, spreading resignation at the march of inevitability.

For Miller, a huge part of his life had ended.

\*\*\*

He sat in the truck at the throat of the cul-de-sac, chain smoking. The night had been warm when he left, but it had turned somewhere past midnight and a cold drizzle gusted outside. Miller didn't mind, it matched his mood and the cold air sobered him. He hadn't smoked in many months and combined with the booze, he was feeling lightheaded. The wind through the driver's window felt like a sturdy, level-headed friend shaking him awake from a stupor.

*Snap out of it, you fool!*

The thought made him smile. He had drunk too much. Even if he were safely at home, it was a lot, much less to be tearing around town and on the highway.

*Jesus, what the fuck were you thinking?*

He shivered, nothing to do with the cold, and took a drag. He closed his eyes and sent out silent gratitude to his guardian angels. He'd made it home without incident.

"God protects fools and drunks," he said to himself.

The wind rose up, shaking against the truck, and Miller took it as sign his offering to the angels had been received. Next came trials of a different kind. He had noticed himself slowing on the highway, then taking back ways through town towards the neighborhood, stopping for the cigarettes. He circled the block twelve times, like a teen cruising for trouble. When he could stall himself no longer, he took the boulevard to their house. As he crested the hill and the familiar grouping of houses came into view, he felt his foot stomp down on the brake and he veered the SUV over to the curb. He had been smoking ever since, staring down at his house. He thought it looked like one in a snowglobe, still and sterile, waiting for another great upheaval to start the snow flying again.

It was after three and all the houses were dark. The rain spattering on the roof of the truck and the hurried gusts of wind had a hypnotic quality to them. Miller felt his eyelids droop, despite the bracing open window. He flicked his dying butt out into the street and opened the pack. He'd smoked seven. Three in rapid succession, which almost made him sick, and now he was averaging one about every twenty minutes. He meant to finish the pack, maybe catch some quick ZZZ-s in the truck. He'd wake up to one of the neighbors or the butt of a police flashlight on his window, but that was small price to pay.

He was getting chilly and the cigarettes were more and more revolting with each puff. The dizzy buzzing in his head was coalescing into a headache and he cursed himself for not buying a water or something when he bought smokes. He didn't relish the idea of waking up sweating and hungover in the truck either. The closer he got to forty, the more he came to appreciate nights asleep in his own bed. The days of crashing on futons or Aunt Lydia's torture device of a pullout were past him. Until Evelyn shooed him to the couch again, that was.

He flashed anger and snatched up another cigarette. He lit it, regretting it immediately, but he was committed now.

*Alea iacta est.*

"The die is cast," he said.

His fury had dimmed quite a bit since he'd pulled over, but he saw it didn't take much to tap back into it. Was it always there now? Had it always been there? Is it possible that it always would be? His head swelled with it. At least it kept the fatigue at bay.

\*\*\*

Miller was fighting sleep, catching himself in nods or roused by the starts of snores. His lungs burned and the urge for water overwhelmed him. Resigning his watch for the night, he reached down for the ignition. A light came on in their house. Miller froze. Had she seen him? He was still well up the hill, too far to see from her angle. Did she see the smoke? Or did she wake to find him still not home?

It wasn't the bedroom light though, nor the bathroom adjacent to it. It was the second floor, the nursery. Miller pulled his hand from the ignition and pocketed the key in his jacket. He sunk low in his seat and stared over the dashboard. Evelyn hadn't even looked toward those stairs since the fall. There was war over moving (*This wouldn't have even happened if you could afford to actually buy us a house!*) – like the stairs in a mortgaged home would somehow be less malevolent than those in their leased hovel. He himself had only been up there a handful of times since the accident, and only to bring things down that he was quietly giving to friends or donating to the Goodwill.

*What was she doing up there?*

His breath caught in his throat when her silhouette approached the window. The curtain parted and he saw her face, peering out into the circle. She'd seen him. Maybe the higher vantage point? He felt certain for a long moment that she was looking right at him. But she made no sign or gave any indication that she could see him. Miller almost admitted his capture and pulled himself up in his seat. Then the shade flipped back and the silhouette retreated from the window.

He reached up and switched the dome lights off so they wouldn't come on when the door opened. Then he slid out of the SUV. He crouched, waiting, rain pattering off his jacket. He eased the door shut, letting it latch on the first catch, and then he gave it a quick shove, sealing it closed. There was a thump, but the sound was eaten by the wind. He hugged the front bumper, hanging low. The light was still on. He looked around. The rain was coming down faster and there were no other sounds. He ran in a crouch, approaching the side of his house like a burglar.

He waited at the edge of his garage. He looked back over the circle, staring at the quiet houses, trying impossibly to see movement in all the windows at once. The rain made flat slapping sounds on his coat, soaking rivulets slipped through his tangles of hair. He hung back, uncertain, listening to the rain. When he was satisfied, he unlocked the door of the garage and darted inside. He leaned on the door to close it and stood in the darkened garage, listening to his quickening breath.

*What the fuck am I doing?*

She was likely back in bed by now, drifting back to sleep. She went in there to mourn or cry or stew and that was that. Good for her. Maybe some closure would help bring her around. And here he was skulking around their garage like a psychopath. There was just something off about it. The sums didn't add up. He had agreed to keep the room like it was (*maybe we'll try again,* and damned if *that* wasn't the wrong thing to say), but she showed no interest in being in there, just knowing it was…what was the word? *Ready.* That was the word; he just didn't like it. There was something quietly insane to families who preserved rooms like that. What if their dead kids really did come home? Dragging up the stairs in slow clomps, the stench of the earth still clinging to them?

His palms had gone slick and adrenaline made his breath come out in a pained whistle. He crossed the darkened garage and sorted out by feel the key for the kitchen. Both of them had lived in the city when they were in their twenties and considered themselves streetwise to a degree. Evelyn had been mugged once and Miller had gotten his car stolen, but otherwise, the mean streets had looked favorably upon them and they reached the suburbs relatively unmolested. He made a token gesture of offering to put in an alarm system for the baby. But his secret plan was to get them a good big dog when Dana was born. Alarm, protector, and nanny in one perfect, slobbering package.

*She's going to be asleep and you're going to scare the living shit out of her.*

He clicked the lock and opened the kitchen door. It made a slight creak and he stopped dead, hanging over the threshold, face pinched. When he heard nothing, he emerged into the kitchen, pulling the door behind him. The damnable squeak happened a second time, but not as loud as the first. The list for groceries hung under a *We Went to Barbados!* magnet. He was tempted to add WD-40 to it.

*All the better to home invade you with, my dear.*

Laughter bubbled up and he had to hold fast to the counter to steady himself.

"Get a grip," he whispered fiercely.

Wouldn't that be something? Evelyn hears maniacal laughter coming from inside her house in the middle of the night. No foul, it's just her hatter husband returned from one of his wild tea parties. The severity of what was unfolding hit him with a sobering crash and he pulled himself together. Sneaking around like this without her knowing was inviting calamity. There was no gun in the house, another war between them, perhaps their most timeworn argument with each other. Miller feared himself with a gun in the house, Evelyn feared everyone else without one in the house. They went round and round. A couple times he smelled the gunpowder in her fingers and knew she'd been to the range. He wondered if she'd squirreled one away somewhere, elaborately hidden out of reach, and thereby useless in an emergency. Again, a dog solved these problems immediately. Miller was sticking to his plan.

He crept around the refrigerator, his footsteps masked by the hum of it. When he met the lip of the linoleum leading to the hallway, he paused. Had he heard something? He took a step and his shoes squished, still wet from outside. He worked his way out of them and rested on the balls of his feet, head cocked toward the stairs. He approached them cautiously, finding new stealth in his stockinged feet. He paused over the first stair. There it was again. A sound. Muffled. A voice.

Hugging the sides to avoid creaks, he advanced up the stairs. At the landing, he waited. There. Laughter. Light, lilting, a sweet sound, contented. It was a sound he hadn't heard in so long, he found himself smiling in its presence. But the laughter wasn't for him. There was the sound of her muffled speech. She was speaking. The laugh drifted down the hallway again, but this time it unnerved him. He was hit with an irrational urge to sneak back downstairs and out and back to the truck and to pull in the drive with headlights blazing and all the fanfare. He'd make a lot of noise with his keys and linger in the kitchen or head straight to the couch and save her the trouble. Whatever it took to give her a headstart at stopping whatever this was and saving face. What was up those stairs was not for his eyes.

His body betrayed him, pulling him inexorably upward. She was talking in low tones, soothing, punctuated with little giggles and nonsense. He approached the light at the top of the stairs with a gathering disquiet. It wasn't whatever Evelyn was up to that made his heart beat faster, it was that it spoke of ritual. This was not the first time she'd been in the nursery. He steeled himself and opened the door.

She turned to greet him, a sunny smile on her face.

"Oh look," she cooed to the thing at her breast. "Daddy's home."

Miller felt the color drain out of his face.

\*\*\*

It was a babydoll, the kind of thing you see in any daycare or kid's room. Blonde curls, planted like corn in rows, sprang through tiny holes drilled into the flesh-colored plastic. The thing stared at him with sightless eyes that he knew, with terrible certainty, would close when it was laid on its back. She-

*It!*

-was wrapped in a puffy pink blanket dotted with penguins. He remembered the day they bought it, fighting about baby names the whole ride home. He suspected that if he were to remove that blanket, it would be wearing the same goofy blue Shirley Temple dress they all wore. The doll's mouth, lips pursed for a nipple, reached towards Evelyn's exposed right breast. Miller felt a scream rising in his gorge.

She was gently bouncing the bundle up and down in her arms. She had been neither surprised by his sudden entry, nor fazed by his expression. Instead she smiled tiredly at him, like a new parent ready to hand the little potato over to their partner for a shift change and some shut-eye. There was a Ward Cleaver, 1950s schlock that saturated the scene so much, he felt like choking. It was loony, laughable. He felt like he'd stepped into a David Lynch movie.

"Evelyn?" he asked, his voice a croak. "What are you doing?"

That same tired smile. The look on her face was such a perfect mimic of a new parent, he half-believed they were actually raising a newborn. How could she have that look down so well? How could she know what that look even felt like, how to emulate it? Had she practiced it? *We're really in this together now and I'm glad I chose you,* that look said. He felt his balls creep up tight and low.

"She couldn't sleep, so I came up."

He swallowed. His throat clicked. The vision in his periphery darkened and for a welcome moment he thought he was going to pass out.

"You're home late."

She was looking at him, but not. She seemed to be running her own script in her head and he suspected it didn't really matter what he said. Evelyn's eyes were as empty as the doll's.

*That's not Evelyn.*

The thought sent a cold spike driving down through to his bones.

*Run.*

"Did you have a good night?"

A simple smile, one of soft adoring.

*Run.*

The thought he had inexplicably gone insane tempted him. He'd feared it all his adult life, was positive he came by it honestly, and this fit the bill in a remarkable fashion.

"Is this really happening?" he asked, voice dry.

She frowned, pouting at him. *Oh silly!* He was going to scream.

"Did somebody have a little too much fun tonight?"

"What's going on here, Lyn?" he felt his voice rising. "What is this?"

"You have to work in the morning," she scolded.

Again, that eerie feeling, the feeling she was running lines for a movie only she could see, gripped him. Could she even hear him? He debated waving his hand in front of her eyes to see if anyone was home. The next thought to tempt him was that he was dead. He had flipped the truck, drunk on the highway and they were scraping him off the tarmac and she couldn't actually see him. He was visiting some cracked-open future where they were happy parents to a beautiful, blonde-haired, blue-eyed babydoll. Any moment now the ghost of Christmas Past would carry him off to his bruised childhood.

"Evelyn," he said sharply.

She drew back from his tone, but seemed for a moment to come forward from behind the mask of this Donna Reed puppet. Her focus wavered, like she was trying to see him and the other him at the same time. He felt acutely like a struggle was going on inside her. Right now, the imposter was in control, but he could see the strain in her face. She wasn't like Donna Reed, she was like Donna Reed with a gun to her head. Smiles too wide. Apple pie too sweet.

"Evelyn," he repeated. "Can you hear me?"

She blinked slowly and seemed to find him, the real him, in her focus. The wan smile wavered and the corner of her mouth worked. She stopped rocking.

"Did you take something?"

The last tempting thought, perhaps the most delicious of them all. Pills. There were a million in the house. Maybe they screwed up her dosage at the pharmacy. Maybe she slugged too many with the wine, he'd seen her do it a lot lately. Another, darker thought rode shotgun with the pills: had she OD'd on purpose? He had never thought of Evelyn as suicidal, even as low as things had gotten for them. But he felt so far away now, standing in this tomb with his wife and a plastic doll, he questioned whether he knew anything about her at all.

"We should try and get some sleep," she said. "She's almost finished."

Back to the script. Miller stared at her exposed breast, at the doll's mouth hovering around her nipple, and had a precarious moment where he was certain the lips would begin to move. The hollow thing would stretch stubby fingers towards the globe of her breast. He would hear the stretching of plastic. Then suckling.

A wiser man, even one simply less stressed, would have asked to hold the baby and then tried to talk her down. But Miller was pushed to his red line, klaxons blaring. He lurched forward and tore the doll from her arms.

*** 

She shrieked and lunged at him.

"MY BABY!"

He pulled the doll up and away from her, trying to keep her fingers from gouging out his eyes. She scrambled for it, face feral.

"STOP THIS!" he shouted.

"NO!"

Her chest was heaving, hair plastered against the sweat on her brow. He backed out of the room, half dragging her, half propelled by her, a dance of frantic limbs. They approached the top of the stairs. He wrenched an arm free and threw the doll as hard as he could down the stairs.

She dove for it, wailing. He wasn't expecting that and he leaped for her.

*Please God don't let her fall again.*

But she wasn't falling. She was jumping. He caught her at the waist and wrestled her to the floor on top of him. She struggled, elbowing him sharply in the ribs, cursing at him. But he held fast and her strength waned. Her breath hitched and then she was sobbing in low horrible cries. He held her, rocking her as best he could, until the storm passed.

Outside, the first light of dawn was breaking over the horizon.

# 12

THEY LAY ON the floor, listening to the birds wake up outside. She had brought his arms up to her shoulders after a time and snuggled into him. The hallway was lightening, run-wild shadows vanquished back to their hiding places behind everyday objects. Her breathing slowed. The coffee maker kicked on downstairs and startled them. They shared a little laugh and a collective tension eased out of them like the gentle passing of a giant animal.

"What's wrong with me?" she asked.

He pushed his nose into her hair and kissed the back of her head.

"There's nothing wrong with you."

She squeezed his forearms against her tightly, like a life preserver.

"I'm sick."

"You're not sick, you're sad."

They were quiet a while.

"I'm hurting, Miller."

She started to cry. He kept his face pressed into her head.

"I know."

"I can't make it stop."

"Hey."

She turned in his arms to face him.

"We need help," he said. "The both of us."

Her eyes welled.

"It's okay," he said. "It's going to be okay."

He hugged her to him and they fell asleep that way, huddled together, foreheads resting against each other like lost children in the forest.

\*\*\*

They woke stiff in the mid-morning and hobbled down to bed. There, they made love for the first time in over a year. It was fine and sweet and welcome. They lay in each other's arms. She stroked his chest, tracing slow figure-eights over the skin. He nestled in her hair. He'd always loved her hair, that dirty blonde Medusa mane, white in the summer and then tawny in the fall. He breathed. Always, she smelled faintly of sand and salt and the coconut sweetness of a faraway island.

This morning, the smell was gone. She was unwashed, and any other time she'd likely be embarrassed, but it wasn't that. They'd once endured a stomach flu together on a trip to Argentina. He remembered the mealy, thick, somehow damp odor of sickness on her, on them both. It was an organic smell, something inherent to bodies and fluids. This was electric. It reminded Miller of the smell the transformers of the electric trains sets used to give off. When you ran the trains too hard or for long enough, that slightly burnt, slightly pungent reek would come out. It was distinctive.

He had a wild image of the Bride of Frankenstein, but it did not bring humor. Only more concern. Had Evelyn run her trains too hard? Was that machine smell because she'd blown a fuse somewhere in there? He continued to sniff her scalp, searching like a dutiful St. Bernard through the snow for a trace of her.

It was easy to lie here with her like this, to drift in the afterglow. By all appearances, it was a lazy Sunday in bed. Under the surface of that, a rekindling of something that had almost been stamped out by loss. And it felt *good*, the feel of her in his arms, the tickle of her fingernail along his chest, the refreshing feeling of newness, like the first rays of sun shining down over a valley after a rain.

But it wasn't real. A shift had happened, as one great epoch shifts into another. It was a changing of the guard, B.C. turning to A.D., smooth as an odometer rolling over. They had seen the age of Evelyn Before. Now, it was the age of Evelyn After. That coconut smell was never coming back. Miller had no idea what to expect in the age of Evelyn After, though he understood that from this point forward, he must remain vigilant and alert.

He was responsible for both of them now.

***

Their first psychiatrist, with a wide, white smile filled with veneered teeth, reminded Miller of Richard Dawson. He peered at Evelyn over his notes, looking at her sharply, but not unkindly.

"So you feel this was more an impulse to save the doll and not a self-destructive gesture?"

Evelyn looked at Miller. He nodded to her. They had coached each other in the truck on the way over to the therapist's office. *They're going to push that button under the desk if they think you jumped on purpose, Lyn.* And her thoughtful nodding, *I know, you're right.* As honest as they were trying to be about seeking help, they agreed some things were safer if they remained private.

"Yes," she paused. "I'm lucky Miller grabbed me."

He squeezed her hand. For Miller, it was a troubling puzzle. If they thought she was suicidal, she would be hospitalized for her own safety. A phone call to the cops and at least 24 hours in a hospital with bars on the windows. At least. They talked about it at length, Miller asking her at one point if she wanted to be hospitalized, to check herself in somewhere. But the idea of being trapped in bedlam with the collective energy of a hundred thousand crazies seeping out of the walls was a nightmare to Evelyn. The one time they'd been to see Miller's mother to announce they'd gotten married had been enough to last her a lifetime. She hotly refused, so they agreed to be careful with what they said. But what if she needed to be hospitalized? He wrestled with his loyalties: to his wife or her well-being?

"And you've both agreed to individual and couples therapy?"

They nodded. He considered them.

"This is an undertaking, something that requires equal participation. A lot of times couples come in here and one is clearly dragging the other. I'll save you a lot of time and money and tell you those couples fail."

Miller looked at her. She squeezed his hand.

"We're ready."

"I'm going to want to start you on some medications."

Miller started.

"Plural?"

The therapist scanned him over the chart and raised an eyebrow, polite accusation in his gaze.

"It's just that she's on a lot of pills already," Miller defended.

The doctor put the chart down and folded his hands over the top. He leaned over the desk and smiled at Miller.

"You're right."

He tapped the chart.

"Some of these pain meds are redundant, so we can just get rid of them. I'm going to trade out your muscle relaxants and Percocet for a mood stabilizer and an anti-depressant. Is that a compromise we can agree on?"

Evelyn's eyes filled with tears.

"Will I be on these the rest of my life?"

The therapist shook his head.

"You use a crutch when you break your leg, see? No shame, no stigma in that, is there? You hop along until you can walk on your own and then you put down the crutch. That's old medicine."

Miller wondered darkly how much of this doctor's time on the links had been paid for by pharmaceutical reps and which Benz in the parking lot was given to him for farming out some new wonder pill to his patients. But his presence demanded his support.

"What kind of side-effects are there?"

He opened his hands out to them, palms up, as if to say: *Well, there's what the box tells you, but here's what we see the most.*

"Weight gain mostly. Loss of sex drive. Changes in appetite and sleep. Those are the big ones. Now there are the black box warnings about suicidal and homicidal ideation, okay. That's something we're obviously going to want to watch for. But it's rare and it's usually just an issue of dosage"

*I'll bet it is*, Miller thought contemptuously.

"Are there any guns in the house?"

Miller laughed.

"Yeah, Lyn's got a bazooka for home invasions," he grinned at them. "Or is it a machine gun?"

Evelyn was silent. Miller stiffened, his grin collapsing. He turned on her.

"Are you fucking kidding me?"

She gulped, eyes locked with the therapist, refusing to acknowledge him.

"Yes. There's a gun."

"Unbelievable," he muttered.

The therapist, smoothing tears in marriages for so long it came as second nature, glided them over this unpleasant patch with the consummate skill of a professional.

"Let's remove those from the house for the time being," he said. "I'm also going to prescribe exercise for you both. You need to move and the partnership aspect of training for something together is good bonding. Pick something you enjoy and set some goals. Have fun with it, but commit to it. A lot of change comes with this step alone."

"Okay Doctor," she said.

Miller nodded grudgingly. The doctor scribbled on a pad and handed it across the desk to them.

"This is a couples and family therapist nearer to you. He does individual counseling also. I trust him and people seem to like him. Doctor Bijay Kendra. Last I knew he was taking new patients. We can call ahead and set something up for you if you like."

They nodded.

"Great," he smiled. "We'll send down to the pharmacy for your prescriptions. Pay attention to how you feel. The medicine builds up over time, so it takes a few weeks to really get a complete picture. Be patient. The mood stabilizer will help. Any other questions?"

Evelyn shook her head. Miller rose and extended his hand across the desk. The doctor took and shook, rising to see them out the door. At the threshold, he put his arms across both their shoulders. The crazy image of Richard Dawson popped back into Miller's head. He seemed about to show them their prize packages. *Okay Vicki, show 'em what they've won!*

"We'll start on the meds and get settled in with Doctor Kendra. Work on what we talked about and I'll see you in a month. Think about that activity you can do together."

"How about the shooting range, Lyn?"

She elbowed him in the ribs. Richard Dawson hustled them out of his office. And things settled down for a while.

\*\*\*

Evelyn returned to work, perhaps the most satisfying rung on the multi-step ladder to their wellbeing. Changes were made to accommodate her. She was offered a liaison role, more administrative with regular hours and better benefits. Evelyn pined, bored and nostalgic about marshaling the floor, but she found command of a different kind in her new position. She was forced to admit she wouldn't miss the late nights and it gave her time with Miller instead of passing him in interludes on the up or down of one of their schedules.

At the suggestion of their new therapist, they took a trip to Turks and Caicos.

"We can't afford it," she insisted, shifting her determined gaze between Doctor Kendra and her husband.

"This may feel like impulse, which is why it frightens you," Doctor Kendra said. "But I assure you it is a gesture that you are doing something positive for yourselves, selfishly and with forethought."

"I know," she said. "It's just not possible."

"Unless…"

Eyes turned to Miller. He was wringing his hands, an expression of pained hope on his face. He doubted he would have had the courage to talk to Evelyn about this one-on-one. Parts of him had been leery about therapies of any kind (his mother was contained, not cured, there was a big difference), but he had taken an instant liking to the soft-spoken Indian. Doctor Kendra was free with kindness and generated an aura of calm authority. *All is well.* Miller and Evelyn had been talking, more than perhaps when they were first dating, and a growing safety net of real trust was knitting them together again. He risked it.

"We set some money aside when we found out about Dana."

She looked up sharply.

"No."

"Come on, Lyn. What are we going to do with it?"

"No," she repeated.

He turned on Doctor Kendra.

"Help me out, doc," he said.

Doctor Kendra tapped his chin, musing.

"There are no sides here," he said. "Though I'd ask you to think about how fitting a tribute it would make to share a wonderful experience after all you've been through."

Miller marveled at him. *Jesus,* he thought. *If I could talk that smooth, I'd get laid all day.* There lay great power in words, Miller supposed. Doctor Kendra passed him a quick glance that said: *I showed her the door, now you're on your own.*

Three weeks later they were lying under the canopy of a giant four-poster bed with the lazy sigh of the Caribbean drifting through the open curtains. The sea swelled and crashed outside their door. Candles flickered, marching intricate shadows across the sheets and canopy. Sated from food and sex and spirits, they lazed under dancing haloes of light, a tangle of sheets and limbs.

"I'm so glad we did this," she said.

"Kids suck," he chanced.

"They're the fucking worst," she said.

Then they were laughing, tumbling, and teasing, until the teasing flamed into urgency and they were tangled up in each other until morning.

***

After some half-hearted and comical attempts at yoga and ballroom dancing, they settled on walking every day with more vigorous hikes when possible. They would meet after work and set out for about an hour. Their circuit took them through their neighborhood, through a dog park, past the elementary school, and then along a riverbank dotted with benches and running trails. Sometimes they'd drive to the shore and hike along the beach or into the hills to hike the more robust trails.

As it turned to Spring, Miller took to jogging, more to his astonishment than anyone else's. Both of them were eating better. They had taken to prepping their meals the night before and came to look forward to their ritual of making supper after their walk and winding down for the night. They had shifted in their weights, Miller losing the ring around his middle while Evelyn filled out the gauntness that had shrouded her.

The nursery had been cleared out and painted over. They sold or donated what was left and repurposed the room as a makeshift workout room. Miller would jack up the volume on the TV to drown out Evelyn cranking out steps on the Stairmaster on those days it was too rainy or freezing to go walking. After lacing up and running his route in the mornings, Miller would crest over the rise of their street and see his house, the sight of that upper window no longer filled him with anxiety.

On days when one or both of them had a tough day, Miller would sometimes run ahead and blow off some steam, either circling back to walk with Evelyn again or resting somewhere up ahead on their route until she caught up. They enjoyed this feature of the walks. There was room for them to be separate, to ruminate and enjoy alone time, while still taking pleasure from the shared activity of the walk. The model for their walks had permeated into other areas of their life together and the friendship between them had deepened.

This particular evening was warm and purple and the sun glowed gold as it sank across the clouds. Miller had been bopping to the radio the whole drive home from work, windows down and sunroof open, singing in a high falsetto to Led Zeppelin. He wanted to lace up and fly, to breathe in that purple dusk, chewing up the pavement as the first of the stars peeked out. And then, returned from glory, he'd feast on mutton and mead, and maybe take his lady by force. He was grinning to himself as he drove too fast over the hill and zoomed into the driveway.

He walked with her for twenty minutes, patient, trading stories with her about the day. But the clouds were a pearlescent white, gleaming gold at their edges, opening up like a flower, blowing out into great white rolls. The breeze rippled through the leaves and he could feel it pushing him. There was a call, like the moon to the tides, to the fleet Mercury in his soul, to fly free.

"-you know?"

He blinked at her.

"Hmm?"

"You weren't even listening to me."

He grinned at her, a bit sheepish, a bit roguish.

"Go, you ass," she said.

He kissed her on the cheek.

"Want me to come back?"

She pushed him off her, laughing.

"I'll meet you at the river," she said.

He kissed her again and bolted. One step lumbering, two steps off-balanced, three to correct, and then he caught his stride and was jogging off towards the park. He felt smooth, he was in tune with the bounce of his feet, the way each step propelled him into the next step. His hip was an axle, swiveling, oiled and responsive. His breath was a sharp inhale through his nose and two quick puffs to exhale. 1-2-3. 1-2-3. When he started breathing in through his mouth, he'd scale it back or slow to a walk.

Tonight he felt like he could run for hours. He bounded across the lawn to the dog park, hopped a small fence, and ran across the open field. A terrier kept pace with him, barking and diving for his heels, and they raced until his owner called him back. Miller kept on, darting across the intersection and past the school. A band was practicing and the sound carried out onto the street. Some people had camped out on the lawn, gathered for the impromptu concert. Miller ran on.

He was winded when he reached the river. He made his way over to one of the benches and sat down hard. He rested his head between his knees and took in great swallows of air. When his heart slowed, he lay with his head back against the bench, staring at the sky. The rippling gurgle of the river was tranquil and there were only a few other walkers and runners on the path. Miller watched clouds float overhead and allowed himself to drift with them, zoning out for a while in the purple dusk.

The rumble of his stomach brought him back to waking consciousness. He rubbed his eyes and yawned. The gold light had bloomed into red and it would be dark before too long. Miller didn't wear a watch, but he guessed he'd been sitting there for maybe twenty minutes. Evelyn would be along soon. He watched the current swirling under the surface of the river, creating pools and eddies that frothed and made small waves. He craved a cigarette, but it had been many weeks for both of them and every time he had one and ran, he regretted it. The seesaw of benefit-vs.-regrets with regards to cigarettes seemed to be finally tipping in his favor.

He tried to lounge more, but he was restless. His stomach rumbled again. He decided to backtrack and pick her up along the trail. Maybe she'd stopped to listen to the band practice. But while they were still hard at work in the band room and there were still groupies stretched out on the lawn when he returned, Evelyn was not among them. Miller continued to the dog park, where he expected to find her glommed on to some awful purse dog like a Lhasa Apso or a pug, cooing over it like it was the cure for cancer. But the park was nearly deserted and Evelyn wasn't there either.

He wasn't worried yet. They never brought cell phones, part of their agreement about the walks. And she'd made fun of him so badly when he suggested two-way radios he never brought it up again: *Uh, Roger Falcon Snowball, are we a go on the Haagen Daaz mission at the corner store? Over?* Maybe she'd just gone home. Maybe she wasn't feeling well and-

*I'll meet you at the river.*

Miller began to run.

***

She was standing only a few steps from where he left her, head cocked slightly, staring up at the sky. She was swaying gently from side to side, like a tall pine on a windy hill. Miller looked around. How many people had driven by her? How many neighbors saw her out here? Why didn't anyone help her? He had left her. *Jesus Christ, I was just sitting on that bench like I had all the time on the world.* He stared at her, guilt threatening to paralyze him. He forced himself to act and approached her, taking her firmly by the shoulders. He shook her, as gently as he could.

"Evelyn," he said.

Her eyes faltered. She shifted her gaze from the sky to him. At first there was blankness, then, like a sudden burst of rain, recognition broke across her face. It was a vision of Alzheimer's, the first tragic draft under the door. *This is what it's going to be like when both of you are old.* He shrugged off the thought. It was too immense to be seen in one image, too painful. She focused in on him.

"Hey beautiful," he said.

Her face showcased a procession of emotions, embarrassment giving way to anger, with fear underlying both.

"Did I zone out?"

He nodded, looking around again.

"Was I out long?"

"Few minutes," he lied. "No big deal."

She was silent a long moment, frowning.

"We'll have to tell the shrink. The dosage is still off."

He shook her again, good naturedly this time.

"We're getting close though, Lyn. It's been a while since one of these. Right?"

She forced a smile.

"You hungry?"

"Starved," she lied and took his arm.

The next day the psychiatrist adjusted her dosage. Two weeks later, Beasley had wiggled into the picture and the incident was forgotten in a blur of all things puppy. But one person remembered. Their neighbor, Noah. He had been on the phone, walking past the bay window in his living room, chatting up a girl he'd met at a show the week before. He glanced out his window to see Evelyn Coretti staring up at the sky. She was vacant, swaying slightly like a scarecrow in the breeze, lips moving, mouthing words to a companion no one else could see.

Even after the police questioned him and new tenants moved into the house across the street, it stayed with him. Years later, sometimes in the night he would wake with a start and shiver in the dark. The sight of her, swaying ghostlike in the dying light, was the most unsettling thing he'd ever seen in his life.

# 13

MILLER SEPARATED THE filets with a slide of the knife. The flesh split apart under the sharp edge, sagging in soft piles on the cutting board. The water was approaching a boil. Time for the pasta. He slid the meat into a sizzling fry pan, bubbling with oil and garlic. The meat hissed, oil popping. He tossed in a spill of his Pinot Grigio and a cloud of fragrant steam filled the room. He lifted the pan from the flames a bit and shook wine around the edges. He lowered the heat and settled it back on the burner.

A slug of wine. *Not too much now, you need to stay sharp.* He picked at some cheese while he waited for the pasta to soften. He took another pull of wine from the bottle.

The texts:

\<should i bring wine?\>

\<bring champagne!\>

\<lol. k.\>

Miller used a spatula to check the meat; it had browned nicely. He flipped the filets and added fresh scallions and a handful of herbs. The pan hissed, sated with the offering, and bubbled content. He turned to the pasta; it folded nicely around his wooden spoon.

"Time for a rinse then," he said.

He reached for the alligator hot gloves Evelyn had gotten him for his bachelor pad back in the day. Steadily, his pirate stash of mementos from his old place kept finding their way to the trash pile, either forced outright or hustled out quietly in the night. But the gloves remained. They were stained with grease and spatters a thousand meals old. The seams had split on the right mitt, exposing the silver spacesuit protective layers underneath. They had been performers in some stellar drunken puppet shows and even featured front and center in an anger exercise with Doctor Kendra. *Well this gator thinks you're being a bitch about it.*

Miller heaved the pot and upturned it into the colander in the sink. He ducked out of the rising steam and turned off the burner, returning the pot to its spot on the stove. With no further need of them, he removed the alligator mitts and threw them into the trash. He rinsed cold water over the quivering pasta and shook the colander. He checked the meat, cutting into the centers with a knife and fork. Perfect. He set the burner to simmer. He glanced at the clock above the door to the kitchen and sent the next text.

<get dressed up too.>

<lol. wow. what are we celebrating?>

<big news.>

<TELL ME NOW! =)>

<they found beasley.>

The wine was tart. He swirled the last of it in circles with his wrist, waiting for her to respond.

<what?>

He snapped his phone closed and turned it off. He tossed it in the trash and then, as an afterthought, reached for his wallet and threw that in as well. Liberated, he went rooting in the fridge for another bottle of wine. He poured himself a glass and stood over the island, relishing the taste of the fresh vintage. He took off his apron and threw it over a chair. He smoothed his tie, rolled down his sleeves, and went out to the living room to search for his blazer.

He clicked on some John Coltrane as he went. Mellow notes rose into the air. He turned off the main lights, including the outside lights. He put on some soft lamps to guide her way, and busied himself lighting candles. Back in the kitchen, he cracked the window over the sink and lit a cigarette. He leaned against the sink and smoked in slow, luxurious drags, staring at the gun on the counter.

And waited.

\*\*\*

The day Beasley was killed had started out like any other, except that Miller had a tough caseload and a site visit that ran over. He was out of sorts and bone tired by the time he pulled in the drive. He had no interest in a walk or a run, only his spot on the couch and maybe a movie. He got out of the truck and heard a whistle. He started, then ignored it and rounded the truck. The whistle came again and he turned.

Noah was waving him over. He looked around, confused, and then crossed the street to meet him. His neighbor looked pale, concerned.

"What's up, Noah," he asked. "Everything okay?"

Noah shrugged, watching him carefully.

"Your wife," he said. "She was out here awhile back having a smoke."

This, in itself was not incriminating, other than her cheating on a pact. He had a little leverage here for something later, not a bad thing to have in the back pocket. But there was more.

"She was all splattered in blood."

Noah rubbed his forearms and wrists. "Like a lot."

Miller turned towards his house. He made to leave, but Noah's gaze held him.

"Said she was cutting up a rabbit for stew and the mess got away from her."

"Okay," Miller said.

Noah stared off past Miller, up the hill. He looked far away.

"I haven't seen the dog around."

Miller put up a hand to wave at him and backed away, irritated he'd even crossed the street in the first place. Keys in hand, he marched back across the circle. Noah stopped him.

"You should be careful," he called.

Miller stopped, then turned on him.

"You remember that day, in the street," Noah forced himself to spit out the rest. "She was spaced out."

"What about it?" Miller demanded.

"She was talking to someone, man."

Noah's eyes were big and he kept wiping sweat off his palms on his pants. He was clearly upset. Unburdened of his secret, he seemed naked. Miller was sympathetic. There had been some strange goings on as of late, he supposed.

"We're going through a patch, Noah," he said. "Thank you for keeping an eye out."

Noah nodded, like he heard what was said, but was determined to press on in spite of it. Miller stopped him.

"Thank you."

His tone was final. He left and turned up the walk to his door. Noah watched after him, deep in thought.

\*\*\*

She rushed into the house, calling for him. He caught her in the front hall.

"Someone found Beasley," was the first thing she said.

He beamed at her and shrugged her out of her coat.

"Isn't it great?"

He leaned in, close to her face, uncomfortably so.

"It's wonderful," she said with a tight smile.

He retreated, taking her coat and hanging it in the hall closet.

"Someone found him wandering across town. They're going to bring him in the morning."

He shook his head at her.

"No champagne?"

"I forgot," she said tonelessly.

He took her hand, leading her down the hall to the kitchen.

"Not to worry," he winked at her. "I think there's a bottle of Cliquot in the cabinet."

They entered the kitchen and he pointed to the table with a flourish.

"For the madame, a steak au poivre with pasta and salad."

She touched the bottom of her throat and swallowed. She looked at him, as if seeing him for the first time.

"You're wearing a tie."

"Your turn," he said. "Why don't you go change and I'll pour us some champagne."

"I…"

"Something fun, like we're back in the tropics."

She hesitated, he waved her on. She stepped slowly out of the room. The cork popped and she jumped slightly. Miller shouted with good cheer and she hurried down the hall.

\*\*\*

He came in to find her curled into a ball on the couch, sobbing. He knelt down beside her, a hand on her shoulders, squeezing her. He got an idea of his surroundings. Nothing seemed out of place, nothing was broken, she didn't appear hurt. But she lurched, sobbing in shuddering heaves, aching.

"Lyn," he put his arms around her. "Hey."

She reached for him and clung to him, crying into the hollow of his lap. He held her, finally settling down beside her. He stroked hair out of her face. She looked at him.

"What happened?"

Her face broke.

"Beasley ran away."

He studied her face.

"I let him out," she said. "He never came back."

He let her cry a while, saying nothing.

"Did you call-"

"I CALLED EVERYONE!" she shrieked.

He recoiled, drawing back his hands from her as if she'd tried to bite him. He rose from the couch, folding his arms in front of his chest, eyeing her carefully. Her breath hitched and she was crying. When she'd calmed, she looked numbly down at her feet.

"I'm going to put up flyers tomorrow," she said.

"Okay," he said hollowly.

"Miller?"

She reminded him of a small child in that moment, a child they would never have.

"Will you stay with me tonight?"

He nodded automatically. She reached for him. He pulled her to her feet and helped her to the bedroom. She washed and changed and at Miller's urging, took some extra sleeping pills, and retired. Miller lingered, taking the chance to snoop the house. He felt ridiculous sifting through their house for clues, but Noah's severity had upset him. He rifled through the laundry and the trash, but saw no evidence of foul play.

*No evidence of a rabbit either.*

He gave up the search after midnight. He poured himself a generous slug of whiskey and watched old science fiction on the television:

*Officer, I'd like to report four bodies in my backyard.*

*Wait right there, Mr. Bennell.*

*How do you know my name?*

*Hang up, Matthew.*
*I didn't tell you my name.*
*Hang up!*

When the long blinks became unbearable, he clicked off the TV and lumbered up to bed. He washed his face, refusing to meet his eyes in the mirror, and climbed into bed with a killer.

***

She returned to the kitchen in a blue dress he'd never seen her wear before. It was the color of the ocean of a warm coast. It was a simple peasant dress, the kind of thing she'd wear if she were off to stomp grapes or pick olives in the garden with a basket under her arm. She'd bicycle into town to pick up some fresh baked bread and they'd dip it in oil and hot pepper in the dying light of a dusty Italian afternoon.

*The last thing I'll see when I die is the ocean.*

She twirled for him. She'd composed herself. He placed a flute in her hand. Crushed into a fine powder, the pills had dissolved quickly.

"You're beautiful."

He raised his glass. "To you."

He downed his glass in two swallows and encouraged her to do the same. He put his hand under the stem of the flute and tipped it up, forcing the liquid down her throat. Her eyes widened, but in one great gulp, she drained her glass. She smacked her lips.

"Ugh," she said. "I think it's gone over, Miller."

"Nah," he insisted, already pouring another round into her glass. "First one's just a gas. Wash it down."

She looked at him like he'd gone crazy.

"Down the hatch," he said and refilled his own glass.

"To Beasley!" he shouted and tipped his head back.

She sniffed her glass, then sipped, tentatively. Satisfied, she took a half swallow and set the glass down on the table. Miller pulled out a chair for her and helped her into it. He filled her bowl with salad and placed it in front of her. The first course laid out, they settled in to eat.

*** 

The next morning had been tricky. Miller was up and out the door early. He'd woken from nightmares and spent the dawn watching his wife sleep, wondering as much as he dared, what kind of dreams were playing in her head. It wasn't until he was well into his workday that it occurred to him he hadn't checked the trash bin in the garage. He dismissed it, refusing to give credence to his discomfort, but by lunch, the idea had gelled into conviction. He begged off the rest of the day, citing intestinal distress (not far from the truth anyway), and spent the ride home in a pensive daze.

He crested the hill, steadily convincing himself he was being foolish, when he saw her car in the driveway. He pumped the brakes and jammed the SUV into reverse, creeping back up the hill and out of sight. Had she called in sick to work? His stomach roiled and an acid burp escaped him. Before he knew what he was doing, he called her office and asked to speak with her boss. From her came disturbing news. Evelyn hadn't been in for weeks.

He snuck down the hill, repeating his mission from the night he caught her with the doll, the tableau somehow more unsettling in broad daylight. He walked, what he hoped was nonchalant and unhurried to the side of the house. He opened the side door and ducked into the garage. His heart thudded in his chest.

The smell hit him first. It was a thick, steamy smell that coated the inside of his mouth and made him gag. He covered his mouth and nose with the sleeve of his jacket and snuck across the garage to the bins on the other side. The smell was stronger here. He froze over the nearest bin, listening for any sounds from inside. If she was in the kitchen, there was only a thin wall and a door between them. If she came out? What would he do then?

Before he could let the thought stay his hand, he pulled off the lid and the smell assaulted him. He reached down to find a plastic bundle. He knew what it was, but a grim part of him needed confirmation. He worked at the knot of the bag as quietly as he could. He unfolded the plastic and drew the bag open. He saw fur. He retched, tossing his head over his shoulder, eyes swimming with tears.

When he got himself under control, he lifted the bundle out of the trash bin as gently as he could. The plastic rustled and the weight shifted in his arms. For one heartstopping moment, he felt it tip and slide and saw the crash happen in his mind. Breathing through his mouth, he carried the plastic bundle to the side door. He waited, sweating, listening for any sounds he'd been discovered. He hefted the sack over his shoulder and locked the door. He walked back to the truck, as fast as he dared without running. He lifted the tailgate and deposited the bag in the back with a grunt of disgust.

It was pungent. His clothes stank of it and he was pretty sure the SUV was done for after this. He produced his phone and angrily stabbed in a phone number. He lit a cigarette and watched his house.

*She was talking to someone, man.*

"Riverside Animal Hospital, how can I help you?"

"I have an unusual request."

\*\*\*

Due to the nature of his request, he was ushered in the back way by a worried looking pair of vet techs. Past the rows of kennels and some isolation chambers, they were met by the same kinky-haired vet who had taken care of Beasley years before. He tried to smile, but her face was impassive. *We take animal abuse very seriously here, Mr. Coretti,* she had said. So he had waited and paced and chewed his thumb while they disassembled Beasley's carcass to find out what had happened. After an hour, the veterinarian returned, fixing him with scarcely contained hatred.

"Beasley was drowned," she said. "He was also torn at, punctured in some places."

She tossed something long and white across the metal exam table at him. It was a fingernail.

"Found in one of the wounds."

She nodded to it.

"I suggest you talk to the police before I do."

He grimaced.

"What will happen to-"

"We'll dispose of the body," she said coldly.

"What do I owe you?" he looked around, pained. "For this?"

"Just go, Mr. Coretti."

He looked towards the exam room.

"Now. Please."

***

After he returned from visiting Gloria, he parked down a side street and texted Evelyn.

<you at work?>

A quick response.

<yes.>

<come home right after. i'm cooking us dinner!>

A pause.

<oh?>

<it's a surprise.>

Another pause.

<should i bring wine?>

<bring champagne!>

He waited until he saw her car pass his hiding spot and then returned home.

***

"Miller?"

Her voice was slurred, like syrup. Her eyelids were drooping and she rocked unsteadily in her seat. She swiped at him across her plate, soiling her arm and scattering food across the table. Her face pinched and she squinted, as if trying to concentrate on a challenging math equation.

"I don't feel so hot," she murmured.

She tried to rise from her chair and staggered. She pulled at the tablecloth to steady herself and pulled down the salad bowl and some of the dinner plates. She swooned and twirled towards the kitchen island like a drunken ballerina or a clockspring dancer whose spring was winding down. She reached for the island to steady herself and missed. She pitched forward into the counter, grasping at the dishwasher for purchase, and pulled the door down on top of her with a crash. She lay still, legs splayed out to either side. Her hands spasmed slightly and her breathing was deep and coarse.

Miller sat and watched her for a long time, sipping the last of his champagne, hating that this was how it was going to end. When he could delay it no longer, he sighed and made himself get up. With a last glance back to his wife, he left to gather his supplies for the long night ahead.

# Act III

"Hey Joe. Where you goin'
with that gun in your hand?
Hey Joe. I said where you goin'
with that gun in your hand?"

-Jimi Hendrix

# 14

HE WAKES WITH a headache. His head feels furry and thick and for a while, he drifts through a half-place where he doesn't really know who or where he is. There is pain at the base of his skull where he connected with the tub, lumpy and throbbing, like a toothache in a giant's mouth. His shoulders ache and there is fiery soreness burning in the small of his back. He tries to curl up and finds that he cannot. As he swims upwards towards the light of consciousness, he discovers he is fixed upright to something sturdy. He struggles weakly against his bonds, murmuring. Gray fog clears and he can feel himself rising up through deep waters. First there is awareness, then pain, remembrance, and finally, with crowning irony, understanding.

Miller is taped to the chair.

\*\*\*

Miller equally appreciated and loathed Evelyn's beauty. In the beginning, when they were dating, she could enflame, even enrage him, with a glance. He saw the heads turn when they were together, how the hum of conversation in a room would change tempo when she entered. She was cool. Surveying. *Women are always shopping,* Charlie would say. Evelyn would hate it, but only because it stung of truth.

Miller considered himself to be shabby. Not lazy. He worked. He had goals and desires. He wasn't as imaginative as he would like, perhaps he could even be considered simple. He did not think of himself as cerebral, but he thought on things deeply. He had not principally excelled in his life, nor had he crashed into rock bottom either. Until he met Evelyn, this seemed to be enough.

It was then the glaring cleanup lights came on and he saw the deep cracks of his flaws. He would never be a smooth man, or an elegant one. He had somehow escaped misogyny and retained manners and carried a dependable and altruistic air about him. But Miller wasn't dashing. He cursed his big nose and stooped shoulders and penchant for awkward silences. The therapy of standup had helped him greatly:

*Dating pretty girls is hard fucking work. You walk into a place and everyone looks at her, and then they see you. And it's like, what the fuck is she doing with you? And you're like, I know man, what kind of crazy-ass Voodoo is that? They're all cruisin' up on her, circling the wagons. Now I gotta learn how to fight…*

He was almost hypervigilant with Evelyn in the beginning of their courtship, studying her, adjusting to her changing moods like a chameleon. He was certain he would lose her somehow, that she was too pretty for him. He had wooed her with bluster, but that reservoir wasn't limitless. The more time he spent with her, the more glaring his cracks became. She had come too soon for Miller. She was a vision of his future, the woman he would grow to be worthy of someday. But he wasn't ready for her now. He felt her, like sand slipping through his fingers.

*You want my advice for dating pretty girls. Just give up, man. You're doing something right, don't change too much or you'll fuck it up. She's gonna catch on anyway, might as well let her and see what sticks…*

This is how it was with Miller and Evelyn. Slowly, like a whipped dog, he had come to accept that she loved him. He relaxed his guard and they came to know each other on a wholly different level. But there were still moments he'd look at her, usually when she didn't know he was looking or when she'd walk into a place she was supposed to meet him, and his breath would catch. What kind of Voodoo indeed.

After the accident, things evened out. Miller hated himself for thinking this way, not for the shallowness so much as the weights and measures of his thought process. The limp and the arm secured his place at her side. He'd seen men stare at her, then notice her gait or some other detail, and she was off the market. Getting rid of cads was easy, just show them someone they have to take care of and *bam!* Off like a shot.

For Miller, it meant he no longer had to bang his chest and hoot at rivals. His wife had slowed, regressed somehow to a level closer aligned to his own. But he felt equal parts creep and jailer, that he had somehow captured her, stolen off with her in the night and locked her in a tower. Was there satisfaction in there somewhere too? If he were being honest with himself? That the tumble had knocked her down a peg – karma backslapping her for cheating on him? For trying to run? *No,* he thought. *No one deserves that.* It just made the match between them more even in Miller's mind.

But he bowed to her beauty regardless, in small subconscious ways. And Evelyn, no fool to her own charms and vanity, knew how to pull his strings. A pout here, a wink there, a finger slowly dragged down her bottom lip. Miller was as much the jailed as the jailer. He wondered if her beauty had blinded him, made it easier to see past the spider cracks that were spreading, made it easier to hold out a little longer to see if things got better.

There is no mistaking it now. He can no longer diminish or deny her. She glows before him, a blush crept high onto her cheeks like warpaint. Her eyes shine. She sits across from him, legs crossed at the knee. Her hair is untamed, ringing a halo around a face that once made him swoon. But no more. The last of whatever made up his wife is gone. The resplendent being burning before him, pulsing with inner pressure, like the fusion of atoms in the sun, is mad.

Miller knows then he is going to die.

***

With Evelyn estranged from her parents and Miller's mother locked into a prior commitment, their wedding was small. It was a simple ceremony on a rocky beach with friends now scattered to the four winds and roughshod homemade vows. They were escorted aboard the cruise ship, waving arm-in-arm as the massive ship pulled out of port. They saw little more than the inside of their cabin for those first luxuriant days. And, holding hands across beach chairs, staring blissfully at the uninterrupted blue of the sea, what she wanted seemed reasonable.

"I'm your wife now, Miller," she said. "I should meet your mother."

He shook his head.

"You don't know what that place is like," he said. "What she's like."

She was insistent.

"Gloria is a major part of your life."

"One I'd like to continue to move past if it's all the same to you."

He was snarky, he regretted it. She smiled at him – *no fighting on the honeymoon.*

"Okay," she relented. "I'll drop it."

But she didn't. She dropped subtle hints and needled him at weak moments, carefully tending the seed she'd planted. They were young lovers, with the promise of a new life together, and time stretched out in all directions. It didn't take long for Miller to give in and in doing so, open the doorway to his destruction.

*** 

"Look, she's nuts, this is what I'm telling you."

They were driving, her hand over his on the shifter.

"Give me another example."

He rolled his eyes. She pushed his shoulder.

"Okay," he said. "You ever hear of a Ford Featherlite or a Takuro Spirit?"

She shook her head. "Are they classics or something?"

He laughed. "They might as well be. They don't exist, Lyn."

She frowned.

"Here's another one. You remember the ad for Bathsuds? The kid is splashing in the tub and mom comes and rubs behind his ear and it squeaks? Then they both look at the camera."

He did his best gameshow face.

"Clean isn't clean 'till it's clean with Bathsuds!"

Her eyebrows knitted at the center of her forehead.

"So, like an alternate dimension kind of thing?"

He shook his hand free of her and put it on the steering wheel.

"Who knows?"

Her hand felt lonely on the shifter and found his thigh.

"Well there's got to be a story in this?"

He picked her hand up off his leg and put it back on the shifter.

"Who cares? Why are you so into this?"

She looked offended.

"I'm trying to understand."

He jerked the wheel and lurched the car over into the breakdown lane. He cut the engine and glared at her. She was startled. He pointed a finger at her.

"Listen to me," he said. "Don't try to understand. You can't."

"I can try-"

"You can't!" he shouted, slamming his fist into the wheel.

They locked eyes. She was defiant.

"Why are you pushing this? Why do you want to meet her so badly?"

She picked lint off her coat and passed him a look he'd never seen on her before.

"I'm going to be the mother of your children. She needs to see that in my face."

He laughed. She arched an eyebrow.

"You don't think I can be a bitch?"

"I have no doubts," he said. "Kind of turning me on, to be honest."

She stretched luxuriously in her seat.

"Oh yeah?" she purred. "You gonna do something about it?"

A tractor trailer thundered past, shaking the car.

"Here?" Miller asked, but he was already unbuckling his seatbelt.

\*\*\*

Gloria Coretti spent most of her mornings in the common room or, if she could get there early enough, the bench at the bay window of the sun room. Captivity had changed her, softening her in some places, hardening her irretrievably in others. Her body had dulled and softened, a sagging testament to a woman she could hardly remember. Decades of forced medication had turned her mind into a rotting cistern, dripping with the damp waters of sedation. She faded in and out, like a faraway radio station. At times she would return to herself fully and rage, violent and tortured, waking from another long dream to find herself in chains. But most of the time she would drift, passing through the halls of the hospital, scenes fading and blending, moments escaping a little at a time like the firmness of an old pillow. She was flat, left folded for hours at a time against other flat inmates, stacked like warped little files in a forgotten cabinet until they died.

Gloria had long ago abandoned thoughts of escape or leniency. She would receive no aid from her son, who had betrayed her and left her in her darkest hour. Her son, hidden from her by press and guardians during the trial, who wouldn't even look at her on the stand. A son who, even now, couldn't take her in fully with his eyes. Miller who, like her, didn't belong here. Whose unique genetic signature, just like her own, was slowly but exponentially tearing the world apart the longer they remained alive. Seeing him was like looking into an open grave.

But this morning, something was different. Gloria knew it upon waking. The air had changed, thickened, and the duty nurse was on edge. Routines were upheld, rounds were performed, but underneath, something hummed. Gloria perched at the sunroom window like a cat, staring watchfully out across the courtyard. Her vigil was rewarded by a flash of blonde hair and the approaching click of heels. The sound was alien and out of place. The slightest whiff of perfume drifted to her nose. Impossible, of course, the click was still far away and behind glass, but Gloria smelled her all the same.

Something wrenched in her, a tugging that was unwelcome, pulling her out of her placid daze with determined arms. She heard them laughing outside and closed her eyes, entertaining an emotion so caked with neglect it was like a rusty axle, creaking in protest. But by the time the guards came to clean her up, the axle was turning freely again, albeit loudly. By the time they chained her to the desk and opened the door, the axle was spinning, rapid and whisper quiet, like a shark circling a meal with a seeping wound.

*\*\**

He approached her, knelt down so he was eye level, and touched her hand. She didn't move, only stared openly at Evelyn.

"Mom," he said. "I want you to meet someone."

He was trying to build a flourish, but Gloria knew what was next. A blonde waif stepped forward on unsteady pin legs, weak pointy things like those of a newborn colt.

"This is Evelyn," he paused. "My wife. We got married."

Rings flashed in her face. Gloria didn't blink.

"Is she pregnant?"

Miller balked.

"Ma-" he started, but Evelyn hurried around him, leaning in to her, like girlfriends sharing gossip.

"Not yet, Mrs. Coretti." She flashed steel. "But we hope to be soon."

Gloria laughed, a sickly wet spasm that drove Evelyn back. Her body shook with it, chains rattling softly. She composed herself and resumed her study of her son's new wife. Miller made small talk, the waif's biography and resume. Evelyn beamed at his cues, a forced affair, her teeth too white and small and perfect. Gloria sent a question past Miller's insufferable prattling.

"Did your stuffed animals talk to you as a child?"

The waif's hand fluttered over her throat.

"Did they ever move?"

Gloria leaned forward.

"I smell death on you."

Miller cut off her gaze with his body.

"That's enough now."

Evelyn murmured something. Miller turned to her, stepping aside.

"My brother died when I was little," she said, louder this time.

A pause.

"Did you kill him?"

Miller drove his fist into the hard metal desktop.

"What the fuck is wrong with you?"

Gloria ignored him. Evelyn's face was pale except for high hectic red marks at her cheeks. Tears spilled down her cheeks and she shook, whether in fear or fury it was impossible to tell. He wrapped his arms around her to protect her and glared at Gloria.

"Go to hell."

She laughed again. Miller signaled the guard.

"You come see me again," she said to Evelyn, choking on laughter. "*When it starts to happen to you!*"

The door buzzed open and Miller hurried his wife out of the room. She was ungainly and he led her back through the maze of hallways to the parking lot. In the car, she trembled and cried. *She's horrible!* And Miller cursed that he could never take back what she knew of his life now. He promised her, solemn and true: *You will never see her again.*

But Gloria lingered.

196

*You come see me again.*

It was turned into a joke between them, perhaps the only way they could move past it. *Oh shit, Miller, I think I'm losing it for real this time, should we tell your mother?* It was just a joke, sometimes funny, oftentimes harmless, but sometimes it was colder. A premonition. Miller wondered about it, if his mother planted a seed of her own that day. If she had spoken not threats, but prophecy. Did Evelyn really fall down the stairs, or had Gloria somehow pushed her? Was this her final crushing wrath against him for running away all those years ago?

*When it starts to happen to you!*

Or did Gloria, made canny by madness, simply sniff out one of her own kind?

\*\*\*

He struggles against his restraints. He is held fast. She has dragged him, lifted him into the chair. How could she have been so strong? But she had superpowers now, didn't she? He laughs to himself.

"What do you think Doctor Kendra would say about this role reversal, Lyn?"

"It's Eve now," she says.

The last of a smile falls from his face like a hanged man through the gallows floor. She is looking right at him, but through him, far beyond him, scalding his retinas with her brightness. He turns his head, breathing hard, twisting to loosen the tape.

"I am Evelyn Prime. The first of my kind. An adaptation. I can animate living matter and manipulate physical laws with my mind."

"Is that what she told you?"

Evelyn scans his face.

"She said I was becoming," she says. "And that you couldn't understand."

Miller stalls for time.

"Then show me, Evelyn. Move some furniture, lift my chair, tear the fucking roof off this place for Christ's sake."

She smiles at him. At one time that smile might be pity, maybe in some part of her it still was.

"I could show you, but you wouldn't trust your eyes. You will be my Adam and we will walk a new world together. But first I have to bring you back."

She raises the gun.

"You have to know."

He bucks against his restraints, pleading.

"Evelyn, don't-"

There are three shots. Miller sees the ocean.

\*\*\*

Evelyn tosses the gun aside and rushes to him. She places her hands at the angry wounds in his chest. There is so much blood. Miller is gasping, spitting up crimson globs. She steadies herself and closes her eyes. She counts her breaths, slowing them down in measures. Her hands, slick with blood, move across Miller's torso, feeling for the first tugging of nerves and tissue under her fingers. She concentrates, pushing all of her focus into knitting the wounds back together.

"Stay with me, Miller," she pants.

He coughs, a reedy wheezing sound. She presses harder, willing his cells to respond to her. And is that a tickle? She reaches in her mind for the medical team, the bustling ER with doctors barking orders. Which artery first? What about his lungs? She lunges through the empty hospital room, knocking over carts and gurneys to find the grizzled attending physician. Under her hands, Miller's breathing is slowing.

*Please God.*

There is a pounding at the door. Shouting. Noah: "I heard shooting! Are you guys okay?" She blocks it out, hands pushing harder, calling to mitochondria and stem cells, summoning platelets and free iron.

"Come on," she demands.

Underneath her, Miller has stopped moving.

"Come on."

Outside the pounding grows more urgent. In the distance, she hears the first faint wail of approaching sirens.

# ABOUT THE AUTHOR

GEOFFREY VISGILIO is the award-winning author of *Believe* (2014), *Switch* (2017), and the upcoming novel, *Leap* (2020). A mix of sherpa, shaman, and shrink, he is an unflinching tourguide into the beyond. A profound spiritual experience launched him on an exploration to the edges of the known. He returned with three books, great humility, and an existential curiosity that is tireless. He is a Rhode Island native and lives in the town of Fog Harbor, where he communes with spirits, both ethereal and distilled.

Visit www.geoffvisgilio.com.